Also By Joseph Ridg.

BURRITO DELUXE

This Book is Dedicated to One of Britain's Most Wanted -
Long May He Run...

-1-

It was a station on the Central Line, it was Monday, and the weekend was about as far away as a distant galaxy hidden in a lost cosmos. I thought about life. Somehow everything disgusted me, like the entire set-up was rotten to the core. All I wanted to do was get away. Mexico. For the last few weeks it was all Ronnie could talk about. He kept banging on about how there was nothing for us in the UK. And really there wasn't. Take my career trajectory - a good example of a dead end street. Since leaving school I'd drifted from one shit job to another, getting fired or walking out before I was fired, and starting all over again. The future loomed up like a vision of doom, stuck in a crap job until I became that job, growing older, passive, and then dying.

A train appeared. The carriages were packed. The carriages on the next train would be just as packed, and so would the one after. This was the commuting life in London. I pushed random people forward and scrambled aboard, my face pressed tight against glass. As the tube hurtled underground I looked at the other workers. They all looked depressed. Why did we do this shit every day of the week, wasting our lives? What was the purpose of it all? What were we doing it for? Where were we going? Fuck it, it was too late for most of them - they were older - in a rut, but I was young with all my faculties intact.

Upon surfacing above ground my disgusted state of mind intensified. I had to find a different way to live - somehow. I walked through a grim East London shopping centre lined with identikit retail outlets until I came to my place of work, a lighting shop hidden in a darkened corner of the mall. I was ten minutes late and Pamela was already there.

Pamela was the manager. I said hello and sat in the chair where I always sat. I turned the radio on and drifted away...

I was in the shadow of a stone tomb, Ronnie beside me, blank expression, unconsciously shredding a hymn sheet into tiny pieces. Nothing appeared believable or real until pall bearers appeared on the scene, holding aloft a coffin, the people watching in silence as the casket was lowered slowly into the earth. In a few weeks whoever was in that coffin would be worm food, in a few years nothing more than bones, and finally dust. Stardust? I liked to think of us as stardust. Beside this grave were other freshly dug graves and in the church was another funeral, one immediately after the other, an endless production line of death.

Ronnie leaned over.

'Soon we'll all be gone.'

The sun set in the west. Mourners drifted away down the hill, figures growing ever smaller, blinding beams of yellow piercing gaps in rows of terraced houses bathing the cemetery in flickering shadows. Leaves swirled and a cold wind blew.

Ronnie knelt beside the grave and offered up a prayer. I didn't say anything and stared into the diminishing sunlight.

'We've got to get out of here,' said Ronnie. 'There's nothing for us here.'

'Where to?'

'Mexico.'

'How?'

'Leave it with me.'

Mexico, Mexico, Mexico... My head fell forward and then backwards with a sudden jerk. Had I fallen asleep and if so had Pamela noticed? I glanced at her on the sly. She was busy filing her nails and perusing a lifestyle magazine. Good. I gazed out of the shop window. People walked past, old and young and then the doors of the shop burst open and two men ran inside. Everything happened fast. A counter hurdle, a kick in the chest, a knife held to my throat.

'WHERE'S THA FUCKING MONEY?' screamed the assailant holding the blade against my neck.

I opened my mouth and swallowed dust. 'We haven't h-had any customers,' I stuttered.

'WHERE'S THA FUCKING MONEY?'

Pamela sat rigid in her chair, face deathly white.

'WHERE'S THA FUCKING MONEY FUCKER?'

Suddenly I was calm. Nothing bad was going to happen. I repeated the haven't-had-any-customers mantra, whilst picturing myself in the bronzed arms of a beautiful senorita. Fuck this cunt with the knife. I was going to Mexico. Then, as if he had read my mind, the robber took the knife away from my neck and signalled to his accomplice that it was time to make a fast exit.

And that was that. The ordeal was over. I touched my neck. Spots of red coated my fingers. I wiped my hand and helped Pamela into a chair.

'You okay?'

'Yes,' she said softly.

Pamela pointed out that my neck was bleeding.

'It's only a nick.'

'Where were the security guards?'

'Where were the police?'

'We were alone, Joseph. They don't care if a shop gets done over.'

As for me I was never working another day in the place. Under no circumstances was I risking my life for the peanuts they considered a fair wage. Anyway I had a plan, another option, a get out clause. Mexico.

'We'll have to call the police,' said Pamela who stood up and wandered out of the shop.

I glanced inside the till. Wrapped inside a plastic moneybag was £250 in petty cash. The unlucky robbers had missed it. I picked the moneybag up, stuck it into my jeans pocket, and walked.

-2-

The government office was a soulless place, overrun with society's rejects, most of whom looked as hopeful of landing employment as they did of winning the lottery. And although the staff employed there actually had jobs they didn't look much better off than their customers.

Eventually I was seen by an advisor, who rambled on and on, some bureaucratic shit I paid little attention to.

'But of course you are not entitled to unemployment benefit.'

Suddenly I was all ears.

'Not entitled to what?'

'Full unemployment benefit.'

'Why not?'

'Because of circumstances.'

'What circumstances?'

'You left your last employment voluntarily.'

'I was held up at knifepoint.'

'Nevertheless, you left voluntarily and actions such as yours are not to be encouraged.'

'Not to be encouraged?'

'Remember, we're all in this together.'

'We're all what, oh shit, who gave you that information, that I left my last job voluntarily?'

'Your previous employer, they said you walked out.'

It was true. I did walk out, free as a bird, but only an imbecile would've stayed.

'You mean it's their word against mine?'

'You could always take the decision to a tribunal.'

'Okay, but before I do that, am I entitled to any money?'

The advisor stared into the monitor and tapped some keys. This went on for some time, during which a fly landed on my ear, and a fight between four women broke out behind me. I considered leaving and was just about to do so when the advisor stopped tapping.

'You are entitled to social funding,' he said and attempted a smile, but thought better of it, curtailing it halfway through.

'How much?'

'£34.56p.'

'Strange amount, what's it for?'

'Essential household items.'

'Such as?'

'Cutlery.'

An hour later I escaped the dingy environs of the social security hellhole, armed with a voucher for £34.56p, which could only be spent in approved government stores. I looked at the voucher and burst out laughing. It was insane, completely nuts. I found an approved government store and walked in.

At the cutlery section I discovered spoons were 75p each. I did the arithmetic. At 75 pence a pop I could afford 46 spoons. I grabbed handfuls of spoons and marched to the counter. I waited in a queue. When the teller saw the spoons and my voucher she adopted an air of barely concealed contempt.

'You want all of spoon?' she asked in broken English.

'Yes, I want all of spoon.'

I walked out carrying a bag containing 46 spoons. Once inside the flat I laid all the spoons on the coffee table. When Ronnie arrived home the spoons were still on the table.

'Lot of spoons there,' he said.

I picked up one of the spoons, breathed onto it, and hung it from my nose. The spoon defied gravity for a few seconds, before dropping to the carpet.

'The sooner we fuck off to Mexico the better.'

'Don't worry I've had an idea.'

'An idea?'

'The Lube gave me the low down in the Pot - the whys and the wheres and the whatnots.'

'He did?'

'Yeah, it's gonna be a piece of piss. We, I mean you, are gonna farm marijuana.'

'We, I mean me?'

'Yeah, from now on Farmer Ridgwell's your name and farming's your game.'

'How did all this come about?'

'Don't worry about how it came about - focus on the fifty thou we gonna clear from the scam.'

'Fifty thou?'

'Twenty five each, enough bees and honey to travel for a year in the style that we are accustomed to.'

I rubbed my hands together. 'When do we start?'

'Tonight.'

A few hours later I was rudely awakened in the middle of the night.

'Go, go, go!' bawled Ronnie.

'Hey, hey, hey, what's going on?' I protested sleepily.

Ronnie ripped the quilt from my body.

'We've got a job to do.'

'What sort of job?'

'All questions answered later, time is of the essence.'

We drove to a row of warehouses in a run-down industrial park. It was 4.00AM. The rattling of machinery exploded into action and a metal shutter moved upwards. Then the head of a black man appeared.

'Billy, yeah?'

'Yeah,' replied Ronnie.

'It's all here, be as quick as ya fucking can.'

A while later we pulled up outside a ramshackle collection of lock-up garages. It was dark. We offloaded the van in record time. Ronnie pulled the door of the lock-up shut and hit the lights. We unpacked boxes and inspected the contents.

'What is all this shit?'

'This, my friend, is all the equipment you're gonna need to become a fully-fledged indoor gardener.'

Ronnie handed me a little booklet the title of which read *How to Grow Weed*.

'What this?'

'That's your bible. All you need to know about growing marijuana in an indoor environment is contained within.'

I put the book down and held an electric light bulb in my hands.

'Massive fucker.'

'Thousand watt, metal halide, used primarily in the vegetative stage.'

Ronnie led me to the back of the lock-up. A fridge was back there. He opened the fridge and pulled out two plastic containers. They looked like baby incubators. The perspex was misted with condensation. Ronnie took the lid off the plastic containers.

'Inside these propagating units are four hundred cuttings of the finest and strongest weed variety known to man. Sourced from Amsterdam and winner of several Cannabis Growers Gold Cups they're a Hindu Cush, Northern Lights, Superskunk combo. These mothers, once mature, contain enough THC to fell a man.'

'THC?'

'The shit that gets all those stoners high.'

It was only necessary to visit the lock-ups once a week.

Growing cannabis in an indoor environment wasn't difficult and my handy *How to Grow Weed* booklet told me all I needed to know. The hydroponics were simple, straightforward; any idiot could do it. Fill the tanks with water, place the cuttings in rock wool and add nutrients. The lights were fixed to timers and the rest looked after itself. In fact everything was running as smooth as a motherfucker until I took Stupid with me. Stupid is my magic cat. She has a problem with balance and keeps breaking her legs. It's a genetic thing. After the fourth break the vet gave me low down, one more fracture and my magic cat would have to be put down. This freaked me out so much that afterwards I only let Stupid out on a leash. Due to her disability I took her out for two walks a day, even when working, in an attempt to strengthen her leg muscles. Oh, and if you want to know why Stupid is a magic cat, it's because she can talk. No one else believes my cat can talk, but she can. It's the way she meows, her mews sound like words. Stupid is black and white with ocean blue eyes.

I hadn't originally intended to take Stupid with me to the lock-up, but the day started out badly when I soaked myself trying to pour a cup of water. The flat I shared with Ronnie was a dump. There were no taps attached to the kitchen sink. Hot and cold water shot straight out of a copper pipe. The valve was touch sensitive, too heavy handed and you got squirted. So that was why I got soaked. Too heavy-handed.

Then I heard a mew. There was Stupid sitting on a worktop, laughing at me.

'Okay fella, for that I'm taking you with me to the lock-ups.'

At the lock-up the luxuriant fragrance of the genus Cannabis Sativa hung heavy in the stultifying air. The plants were in lush condition, an abundance of green leaves attached to vibrant standing to attention stems. I took out a pH meter, measured the level of nutrients in each tank, and adjusted them to optimum levels.

As I did all this Stupid explored the place, fascinated by the aroma emanating from the plants, holding her nose upwards, sniffing the air continuously. Then she clawed a large green leaf from one of the plants and stuffed it into her mouth.

Just as I was wondering if a cannabis leaf could do long-term damage to the health of a cat, even a magic cat, the sound of a car pulling up brought me to my senses. I crept over to the door of the lock-up and pressed my ear against cold metal. Outside, voices, two men talking.

'These'll do nicely.'

'No one using em?

'Na, derelict.'

Panic waves. The door to the lock-up was open. If anybody lifted the thing the extent of my dodgy criminal activity would be revealed. Shit. I switched the lights off; in fact I switched everything off. The voices continued.

'Off to the next lot?'

'Yep.'

Footsteps crunched. Car doors opened and clunked closed. I broke out in a cold sweat. A car engine spluttered into life, wheels on gravel, loud, and then fading away...

Forty-eight hours later I awoke from a drunken stupor and scanned my bedroom with ye old bleary eye. It had been another big Friday night, starting out in the Pot, then Neons, and finishing back at the flat around black-out time. Aside from the hangover of death something was wrong. There was a can of beer on the bedside table, left over from the night before. I grabbed it, a quarter full. I downed the warm liquid and began remembering stuff, specifically long brown hair and a pair of thigh length leather boots. I inspected my bed. On the pillow was a nest of brown hair and several smudges of foundation, mixed with a little pink lipstick. Had a girl been there?

Then I realised my head was cold. I touched my bonce all over. Where the fuck was Stupid? As my magic cat made a habit of sleeping on my head every night it felt wrong without her warm fur resting there. I made a frantic search of the flat.

'Stupid, Stupid, Stupid.'

No response. I looked out to the garden. The weeping willow swayed, a pigeon flew past, but no sign of a disabled feline. Had she somehow escaped?

The door to Ronnie's room was shut. I rapped the wood. No answer. I rapped again, louder. A muffled response.

'What?'

'You seen Stupid?'

'No.'

I wasn't satisfied and barged the door open. Inside, a dirty blonde sat up in Ronnie's double bed, a makeshift futon thing that he'd made out of wooden pallets. The girl was reading a battered copy of Gregory Corso's *Gasoline*, topless. Ronnie was a genuine lit fiend - a great fan of forgotten London classics and the Beats, especially the mythology of it all, and his bookshelves were filled with that type of literature, Curtis, Hamilton, Kersch, Ginsberg, Bukowski, Kerouac, Burroughs, Synder etc. He was also a great collector, first editions, rare paperbacks and chapbooks, even the odd broadside. It was how we'd got together in the first place. We'd met in our local library in East London. I'd been holding a hardback edition of *Visions of Cody* by Jack Kerouac when he approached and started talking about literature, art, music, survival on the streets, and future plans. Liking all the same authors we immediately clicked and from then on were best friends. Later, when we found our beat apartment, it went without saying that we would live together and do everything together from that day on until we grew old or got married or affected by some other adult event which usually gets in the way of best friend relationships. Like me Ronnie was a born and bred Cockney and like me he wanted to escape from the Capital's mean streets and tread more colourful and exotic thoroughfares. For as he often told me - there's a big wide world out there and I want to see some of it before I grow too old. Ronnie was always full of interesting ideas and passionate about everything. And when he said he'd do something it was odds on that he would - no matter how unlikely or fanciful the idea was. He also had these powerful different coloured eyes, one blue, one green, that possessed something hypnotic about them. They were small eyes - set into a bony face, which when looked into had a strange effect that was not easily explained by those who felt their power. And when we've done all our adventuring - Ronnie would often say with a gleam in his strange eyes - we'll come home and write books all about it - and the madder and crazier our adventures - the madder and crazier our books will be.

'Hi,' said the girl languidly.

I eyeballed her tits on the sly. They were a nice pair, just over a handful. 'Seen a black and white cat that can't jump?'

The girl pulled the quilt over her breasts and flicked a page of *Gasoline*.

'She ain't been in here,' said Ronnie, who was occupied in the construction of an extra large spliff. 'What about you last night?'

'What about me last night?'

'Ya don't remember do ya?'

'Give me the low down.'

'We came back here, with Nicole and her mate.'

'Her mate?'

The blonde gasped, looked to Ronnie, and then back to me. 'Ow drunk was ya? My mate, my best friend Katie, the girl you said had starry skies all around her eyes.'

'Long brown hair, proper sort potato?'

'Er, yeah.'

'Wearing black thigh-length leather boots?'

'So, you do remember?'

'Na, can't remember a thing,' I sniggered.

Ronnie sniggered. 'And do you remember putting on them boots and then bowling in here about three o'clock in the morning?'

I rubbed my chin, I stared at the ceiling and then, 'Na.'

'Nothing else on though geez, telling me an Nicole here that we had to stand and deliver.'

Nicole burst out laughing. 'Looked like Dick Turpin in his birthday suit.'

'So where is she now?'

'Where d'ya think? After your highwayman impression you put on Elvis's greatest hits and crashed out sparko. Katie took one look at you, lying there snoring and called a cab. She was pissed off she didn't get a shag I can tell ya.'

Ronnie cracked up at that.

'Easy, easy,' I said, 'forgot all that crappola, I still can't find me magic cat.'

Ronnie licked one length of a king-size paper.

'When was the last time you saw her?'

When was the last time I'd seen Stupid? Then a moment of clarity. The lock-up.

'Shit, I think I left her in the you know where.'

'In the you know what?'

'See ya.'

Ten minutes later I was outside the lock-up, opening the door with shaky hands. If anything had happened to Stupid because of my carelessness I'd never forgive myself. Seconds later I was in. Everything looked the same, lights on, water trickling in the tanks, plants flourishing. Good. I scanned the grow room and there was my pet, sitting in a corner. She mewed, reached out a paw, clawed a lush green leaf, and shoved it into her mouth. I looked at the plant nearest to my cat, two thirds eaten. And if it was possible for a feline to look stoned, Stupid was gone, high as a kite and then some.

'Come on, let's get you home,' I said tenderly.

As I cradled her in my arms Stupid mewed some more, but none of it made any sense, pure spaced-out gibberish.

A few weeks later everything was going well, in fact everything was running so smoothly that Mexico began to feel like I could reach out and grab it. Then it happened. It was a week before harvest time. The first thing I noticed was the smell, a disconcerting aroma, like death or the stench of rotting corpses. I remember opening the doors to the lock-up with intuitive apprehension. My first thought was that some animal or rodent had crawled inside and died. I'd arrived during the night cycle, the grow room bathed in darkness, and aside from the sound of running water, the room was eerily silent.

I flashed a torch beam across the plants. In the wavering light they looked wrong, limp, hanging down, instead of reaching skywards. Black clouds hovered around each plant. I flicked the fan switches on and off. Nothing happened. Shit. I shone my torch on the timer switches. Turning the lights on during the night cycle was an indoor gardening no-no, but something needed to be done. I snapped the switches and flickering orange lights flashed here and there.

As my eyes adjusted to the new lighting conditions, the problem revealed itself. It was a massive fucking problem, in fact a disaster. Each plant covered in a layer of luxuriant mold, the leaves dusted with green powder, the stems encased in lush green velvet. I tapped a leaf nearest to me and a cloud of green dust rose into the air. I inspected a large bud. It was completely covered in mold, nothing more than an empty husk.

And then there were the black clouds, hordes of little flies, swarms of the fuckers, of biblical proportions. I checked the fans. According to the timers they had stopped working at exactly the same time, a freak occurrence.

The extractor fans ensured humidity in the room remained at optimum levels, ensuring healthy growing conditions, too much humidity or too low and any indoor gardener experienced problems. With the fans out of action humidity levels had soared. A drop of water landed on my nose. I looked up; the ceiling was covered in condensation, warm water dripping everywhere. I leaned against a wall and stared at the devastation in utter dismay.

After assessing the damage I got to work. There was a trouble-shooting section in my *How to Grow Weed* handbook, and I frantically flicked the pages. Yes, there it was right at the back: mold and insect infestations.

Both were common problems when growing in an artificial environment, high humidity and lack of decent ventilation major contributing factors. Those damn fans, how they fuck did they stop working at the same time; I mean what were the odds? A hex, that was it. Somebody or something had put a hex on me.

I dealt with the mold by carefully washing every affected stem with warm soapy water. Underneath the plants didn't look so good, blackened and weakened, unable to support themselves. Once the mold was taken care of I set about replacing the broken fans and getting hold of some industrial strength insecticide. A short while later I left the nearest DIY store armed with both. On the way I thought about Ronnie. What was I going to tell him? Even if the plants recovered, at least fifty percent of the crop had been decimated. In the end I decided to wait a few days before mentioning anything.

After fixing the fans and spraying the crop with insecticide I returned to the flat, worrying and fretting all the way. In fact, I even went so far as to say a prayer. I doubted there was a God, but if there was, I called upon the fucker.

'Dear God, I don't go to Church or the Mosque or Synagogue, or any other place of worship aside from for weddings and funerals, but if you are looking down on me and you are indeed omniscient, please find it within your heart to let the rest of the harvest be okay so I can get the fuck out of London and go to Mexico.'

Crazy shit like that. I held out zero hope of my prayer working, but desperate men do desperate shit. Back at the flat I acted like everything was normal.

'Everything sweet?' said Ronnie.

'Sweet as,' I replied, but sweet it was not.

Afterwards I checked the crop each day, but no matter what I did the situation continued to deteriorate at an alarming rate. The mold was an especially virulent kind, a super mold unknown to modern science. Each time I washed the green shit from the plants, it returned the following day with a vengeance. And even the flies remained undefeated. I sprayed copious amounts of insecticide and their bodies littered the grow room but they were irrepressible, always re-grouping and coming back for more.

A day before harvest I broke the news to Ronnie.

'What?'

'I've tried everything, but nothing's worked.'

'When did all this occur?'

'A few days ago.'

'And why have I only just found out?'

'Didn't know what to do did I? I was in shock.'

'You were in shock, how d'ya think I fucking feel?'

'It's a nightmare.'

'How much d'ya think we've lost?'

It doesn't look good.'

'How much?'

'Over seventy percent, maybe more.'

'Blimey.'

I took Ronnie to the grow room and showed him the damage.

'I can't fucking believe it,' he said after a rapid assessment of the devastation.

'We can kiss Mexico goodbye, at least for another year that's for sure.'

Ronnie walked around the plants, inspecting each one with a look of disgust. 'I don't think I can wait that long, and what if it happens again?'

'What's the odds?'

'Long fucking odds, but it's not beyond the realms of possibility.'

'What else can we do?'

'For now it's damage limitation. Dry what's left and offload to Surfer Boy. Accept nothing less than a bag of sand.'

Surfer Boy shifted what was left of the harvest to some rich kids in little under a week. When he told me the posh fucks couldn't get enough of it and asked where could get his hands on some more, all I could do was wince. We cleared nearly a grand profit in total, and would've cleared fifty thou easy if not for the super mold infestation of death. Strangely, Ronnie was pleased with the dispiriting outcome.

'At least we ain't down. This is a very important point because profit, no matter how small, is still profit.'

-3-

I was in Pearl's café. Pearl's was just around the corner from my beat apartment, and it was warm and cosy and Pearl was dead.

The café was done up like a Parisian bistro, red and white checked table cloths, stucco walls, wooden beams, candles in wine bottles. Pearl's daughter ran the place single-handed. Ava was in her early forties and still a looker, but back in the day she'd been a heartbreaker, just like Pearl. There were photos of Billy Fury all over the walls. Billy Fury was Ava's teenage idol and often his music could be heard on the sound system, *Halfway to Paradise, Maybe Tomorrow, Collette, Last Night was Made For Love, Jealousy*.

In those days Ava was a great listener and I used to tell her everything. She always encouraged me to chase my dreams and I trusted her without question. When I told her about my plans to go to Mexico she told me this:

'This place sucks the life out of ya, best thing to do is get out while you can, while you're still young I mean.'

Once, when drunk, I scrawled a poem on one of the café's napkins. When Ava read it she let out a shriek and said it was beautiful and afterwards had it framed and hung on the wall next to a photo of Billy Fury in his fifties rock and roll heyday. I went to Pearl's café three or four times a week. Often, after a few glasses of vino, Ava talked about her husband. They'd met in school, teenage sweethearts, the first and only time she'd been in love. It was love at first sight, she said. He died of a brain tumour at thirty-nine years of age. At the funeral Ava swore she would never marry again and she'd been true to her word. I called her the last of the romantics.

'Life's not fair, Joe Boy, it's all a load of bollocks,' Ava would tell me once she was onto her second bottle of wine. 'If anyone tells you any different, they're liars. There is no God and there is no heaven.'

I think it was the way she said them, but I've always remembered those words.

So there I was in Pearl's, talking about my girlfriend. The relationship was in trouble and things had to change. I'd been seeing Angel for about a year, but for the last few months all we'd done was row, split-up, make-up, and row again. As far as I could see Angel wanted one thing and I wanted another.

As usual I was the only customer in Pearl's. There were rarely any customers, but that's why I liked it. So there was just me and Ava, oh and Stupid, who was sitting on a window ledge watching the world go by, her tail hanging down like a furry umbrella handle. Ava listened patiently to my life problems.

'So Ave, what d'ya think is the best way to go about it?'

Ava flicked cigarette ash into an ashtray and took a sip from a large glass of red wine.

'And your mind's definitely made up?'

'Yeah, it's do or die, o Solo Mio.'

'Best to nip it in the bud then, tell her face to face, don't let her find out from someone else.'

Ava was only telling me what I already knew. Things couldn't go on the way they were. Angel needed to be told. I swigged the rest of the beer and slammed the bottle down hard on the table.

'Fuck it, you're right Ava. I'm gonna do it. I'm gonna do it tonight, in fact right now.'

'But be careful, sweet as Angel is, she's got one hell of a temper on her.'

In some respects Angel was one of the loveliest girls I'd ever met, but she'd been spoilt rotten as a child and was used to getting her own way. If she got her own way everything was hunky dory but if she didn't, well, you had to be careful.

'I will, but it's got to be done. Carrying on like this isn't fair to either of us. Anyway I'll be off to Mexico and she'll forget all about me.'

Before leaving I took another beer for Dutch courage and put Stupid on her lead. As I made my way out Ava winked.

'And remember, you'll always have me.'

'Yeah,' I replied without thinking, but outside I stopped dead. Remember you'll always have me? Ava was a bit of a flirt, but she was nearly twenty years older and shagging Tony Baloney, a well-known local gangster.

I dropped Stupid off at the flat and borrowed the community Volks to drive over to Angel's. When I told Ronnie about my mission he just shook his head.

'That'll be the day. That bird's got you wrapped round her little finger.'

Fuck him. Does he think he's John Wayne? I'll show him, I'll show Ava, I'll show Stupid, I'll show Angel, I'll show everyone. On the way to Angel's I stopped off at an offie and bought two bottles of vino. After six beers at Pearl's I had a taste for the booze and reckoned a good toot might help in the break-up.

The response I got when Angel opened the door and saw me standing there was this:

'Oh, it's you.'

I raised the vino.

'Fancy a drink?'

'Yeah, yeah.'

It was late and Angel was watching television, sprawled out on the sofa, dressed only in a tee-shirt. Three months into the relationship she'd landed some high-flyer number in the city and the job had driven a wedge between us. Angel began to envisage more to life than getting drunk in local boozers, shagging, and talking shit about poetry that I was yet to write. Maybe that was why I wanted to break-up. Maybe I was scared of getting dumped, scared of rejection. Not that Angel was interested in rich guys; she found them a turn-off, too much in love with money and themselves. And it wasn't that I was ugly, but she didn't even go for the handsome dudes. Those pricks are far too vain and looks fade, said she. And then what are you left with? She was only twenty-two, but Angel knew what was going on in the world and was wise beyond her years.

I handed her a glass of chilled plonk and for a while we sat in silence, watching some shit on television, and wondering. I don't know what Angel was thinking, but I was concentrating on the best way to break the bad news. It was odds on that Angel would be seriously fucking pissed off. For one thing it would annoy the fuck out of her that she hadn't dumped me first.

Angel gazed in the direction of the television screen.

'So where ya been?'

'Pearl's.'

'Why the fuck d'ya always go there?'

'It's nice and quiet and Ava lets me take Stupid inside.'

'What is it with you and that old crone?'

'Old crone, she's not an old crone. Anyway I like her, she gives good advice.'

Angel took a gulp of white, wiped her lips, and glared at me.

'Are you sure that's the only thing that pensioner gives ya?'

I sipped my vino and remained silent for a few seconds. This was typical of our recent interaction. What happened to the free and easy conversations we'd shared back in the early days, when we could make each other laugh without trying, when we found each other endlessly interesting?

'What exactly are you insinuating?'

Angel downed the rest of her vino and slammed the glass onto a table.

'I'm insinuating that maybe she sucks ya cock as well as gives advice.'

'Ooh, that's gross Ang.'

'Bullshit. Look. I'm going to bed. Some of us, those who are not bums, have work in the morning.'

'What about the vino?'

'Drink it yourself; it's the one thing you're good at.'

'Listen, there's something I need to tell you,' I said softly.

Angel turned around, slowly. 'Something you need to tell me?'

'I think we need to break-up.'

'You think we need to do what?'

'A break, like a break-up, just for a trial period.'

At first Angel was confused, like the words were beyond her comprehension, but that didn't last.

'YOU FUCKING BASTARD!'

Angel went mental, screaming and hollering like a banshee. I shouted and hollered as well, but about relationship issues, feeling unloved, unwanted. Then Angel rushed me. Instinctively I dropped to the settee and covered my head. The blows came fast and furious, but lacking power, it was like being hit by a child. Then, unexpectedly, everything stopped. All I could hear was sobbing. I opened one eye. Angel had both arms wrapped around my left leg.

'How could ya do this, after all I've done for ya?'

'It's no good Ang, it's over.'

Angel strengthened her grip on my left leg. Shit, it felt like a python was down there.

'No,' she wailed.

I stood up and tried to make it across the room. 'Yes!'

'No.'

By now I was dragging Angel bodily across the room.

'This is ridiculous.'

'No,' sobbed Angel.

I reached down and prised the clam-like arms away from my leg and made it to the doorway. I turned around. Angel lay on the floor like a dying swan in a Tchaikovsky ballet.

'I'm going.'

Angel looked up from her prone position. 'Going?'

'That's right, it's over.'

Angel narrowed her eyes until she looked like a Siamese cat. Then she jumped up defiantly, her sense of pride restored. In fact she looked stunningly beautiful.

'Fuck off then ya useless piece of shit. I only wanted ya here for a shag and there's plenty more waiting to fill your boots.'

I baulked at this, but it was certainly true and some of those pricks probably had decent jobs. I hesitated.

'GET THE FUCK OUT BEFORE I CALL THE POLICE!'

-5-

I awoke Sunday morning with a blinding headache, disconnected from everything. Stupid was nowhere to be seen, but a nest of hairs on the pillow indicated she had slept in her usual place. I checked the time, four-thirty p.m. Where the fuck had the weekend gone? I walked into the bathroom to shower. Whilst showering I noticed some writing on my hand. I switched the shower off. The name had all but disappeared, the number barely legible, but certain events were clear in my mind. Friday night and a girl called Cherry. It seemed another lifetime ago. I dashed into my bedroom and punched the number into my mobile before it disappeared forever.

Ronnie was nowhere to be seen, his bed undisturbed. I remembered him leaving a pub with a girl sometime on Saturday, but those details were shrouded in a booze mist. I went to the kitchen and fixed some pasta. Stupid was in the living room, observing street scenes from the windowsill, every so often her tail twitching when she saw a bird or something. I watched television and ate the pasta in a zombified state. Then I found a can of Stella, had a hair of the dog, and wondered if I should give Cherry a call.

Two hours later Ronnie hadn't returned, and bored, I hit Cherry's number.

'Didn't think you'd call.'

Images of a no-strings attached shag floated through my come-down mind.

'Fancy meeting up?'

'Yeah, why not, ya can come round mine if ya want.'

We arranged to meet later that evening.

Cherry lived in a run-down sink estate that made the

dump I lived in appear positively salubrious. A group of hoodies hung around a broken public telephone box and when I passed by one of them blew a raspberry, which although unthreatening in itself, caused me to flinch. The kids burst out laughing and I cursed myself for being so jumpy.

I located the block Cherry lived in and rang the bell to her flat hoping she was good looking, but as soon as the door opened all my hopes evaporated. I contemplated a super fast, yet at the same time discreet exit, but it was too late.

'Hello.'

'Come in.'

Cherry had a pretty face and warm disposition. I saw how it all worked. In the gloomy environs of the warehouse, and under the influence of booze and narcotics she had appeared as the epitome of female perfection. I cursed those beer goggles. They always distorted the truth and twisted reality. Not once had they given me a pleasant surprise.

The council flat was a cramped affair, sparsely furnished, depressingly bleak. As I stepped inside Cherry asked me to be quiet.

'Why?'

I was led to the only bedroom. Beside the bed was a small wooden cot, lying inside of which was a baby no more than a few weeks old. Sleeping peacefully, the infant looked like a waxwork doll.

'She's asleep.'

I said nothing, but Cherry read my mind.

'It's not mine, I'm babysitting for a friend.'

Instantly I envisaged the scenario. A mate impregnated in her teens. The dad had done a runner, and now the girl would spend the next few years getting people to look after the thing so she could lead a normal life. Council estate chic.

Once the baby revelation was out of the way we gravitated towards the living room. Another drab affair, cheap leather settee, rental television and DVD player. Placed on a badly constructed cabinet were photographs of the baby and a retarded looking mother. I kept sizing up Cherry. She was huge, not overweight, but obese. Again I wondered, for even with the beer and drug goggles it was inexplicable.

We sat on the settee together. Cherry asked if I wanted to watch a film.

'What ya got?'

She fumbled through what looked like a really lame collection and then held up a DVD case.

'Have ya seen this?'

'Na.'

Cherry put the film on and we settled down. She sat with a large cushion on her lap, but the tactic didn't work – she was still huge. She asked if I would like a drink. All she had was a couple of bottles of Smirnoff Ice. She handed me a bottle. It was lukewarm. As she walked across the room I discerned a pronounced limp. I was going to ask about the limp, but something stopped me. We sat supping our sugary alco-pops and watched the film in silence.

The movie was terrible, preposterous plot, lacklustre acting, combined with a predictable Hollywood ending. At some stage Cherry moved closer. Light emanating from the television covered us in flickering shadows. In the dark Cherry was pretty. She really did have an attractive face, large black eyes and glossy eyelashes.

The film went on forever and I began focusing on when to make a move as I didn't want to be there all night. At the film's end we sat and talked. When the last of my Smirnoff Ice went down the hatch I decided to kiss Cherry, but on leaning over she flinched.

'You alright?'

Cherry told me straight out, no hesitation and my weekend was over.

'I've got a false leg.'

That explained the limp. The silence resonated. The television continued to flicker, DVD PLAYER in white letters bouncing in diagonal directions. Maybe it was the silence or more likely my stupid face, which encouraged Cherry's confessional mechanisms. I wasn't sure, but she fed me way too much information for a first date or second, third or fourth for that matter.

'It was my mother.'

Still I didn't say anything, I had transformed into a mute.

'She was Chinese. I was born in New Zealand. My dad's Polynesian. None of it was my mum's fault, it was her family.'

Chinese, Polynesian, New Zealand? Why was she telling me all this and why now? All I could do was nod my head.

'My mum got pregnant out of wedlock. She was only sixteen and in those days it was a scandal. And even more of a scandal when they found out my father was Maori; they were really racist about it.'

Unable to respond I remained in mute mode, but as soon as the confession was over I was getting the fuck out of there, pronto.

'They disowned her and she tried to get rid of it. I mean me, she was just a kid.'

Finally I found I could speak, but Oscar Wilde it wasn't.

'Huh?'

'Yeah, she stuck a knitting needle inside her, thinking it would kill me, but it didn't. I survived, but it messed up one of my legs. Her family couldn't deal with it and put me up for adoption. Shortly afterwards my real mum committed suicide.'

I couldn't deal with it either.

'I was adopted by an English couple. I came to England when I was four, that's why I don't have an accent. Look it happened, but I'm alive and I've got a prosthetic leg.'

Cherry told the story like it was everyday occurrence, but it wasn't, it was a total tragedy. We kissed some more and the thought of what it would be like to fuck a bird with one leg, an amputee, flashed through my mind. The images turned me on, but the kisses went nowhere. Eventually we stopped.

'I've got to go,' I said.

Cherry was relieved.

'Yeah, it's getting late and my friend should be back soon.'

I made my way to the door. On the threshold I gave Cherry a peck on the cheek.

'Will we see each other again?'

'Yeah, I'll give you a bell,' I lied.

'That would be nice,' were Cherry's last words.

I walked home in a daze. At the start of the weekend I'd felt powerful, like anything was possible, but now I felt like a bag of shit. The gang of kids had disappeared, but the broken telephone box remained, the receiver hanging to the ground like an umbilical cord, fragments of glass scattered across the pavement like broken dreams. I thought about Cherry's teenage mum trying to kill her own baby by sticking a knitting needle up her cunt because her parents didn't approve of her relationship with a Maori or sex before marriage, or some other prejudiced shit.

Aside from a kebab restaurant, all the shops in the high street were closed and rubbish was everywhere, a dirty reminder of the weekend. I stuffed my hands into my jean pockets and walked on, head bowed to the wind.

-6-

On Thursday I was back in Pearl's café. Ava was pleased to see me, her smile radiating warmth. Straight away I knew something was going to happen. It had been building up for months. I let Stupid off her leash and sat down at my favourite table where I always sat.

'I've had a bad experience Ave,' I stated dramatically.

Ava came over with a bottle of Rioja and poured two glasses. She sat next to me.

'Is it anything to do with Angel hooking up with Tony?'

After the break-up with Angel the disturbing rumour doing the rounds was that my ex was now shagging local gangster Tony Baloney, a serial womaniser, and a bit of a hard bastard.

'What? No way. Me and Angel are over, finito. From now on she can do what she wants, but why she's with the Sausage Man is beyond me.'

A distant look appeared in Ava's green eyes. 'Yeah, it is strange... so what was the bad experience?'

I took a swig of vino and noticed Ava's thigh touching mine. I had to concentrate on not getting a boner. Shit, I had to fuck her brains out.

'No nothing to do with that, thank God, it's just I met this bird...'

As we drank the vino I told Ava all about one-legged Cherry and her sad tale and how I felt guilty at not calling or seeing her again. Ava sidled closer, leaning across me as she spoke.

'Well you shouldn't feel guilty, not your fault was it? Just remember that certain events and actions are beyond our control and there's nothing we can do about them. Shall we open another bottle of Rioja?'

Before answering Ava looked me in the eyes and winked. It was then the connection was made. It was now only a matter of time.

'Why not? Let's drink to the sadness of life.'

Halfway through the second bottle Ava played some Billy Fury on the stereo, *Halfway to Paradise.* I don't know if she played that song on purpose, but I reckoned paradise was only one or two drinks away.

'I feel tipsy,' said Ava.

'Me too,' I said.

And then we were kissing, in Pearl's Cafe. Fuck, even Stupid was shocked. Ava grabbed my hand and led me upstairs and into the bedroom...

The next morning my head felt like it was about to explode. I lay there suffering and wondering. It all seemed surreal, unbelievable, me and Ava lying in bed together after a night of passion. The strangest thing was that I'd forgotten about Stupid, but of course she hadn't forgotten me, and was happily sleeping on my head.

I nudged my magic cat aside and gazed at Ava. Sunlight streaming through a gap in the blinds did her few favours, making her truly look her age, each and every wrinkle highlighted in blinding yellow, the cellulite on her thighs dappled like the peel of an orange. A wave of nausea hit me. Then there was last night, the four bottles of vino and the sex. Ava had been insatiable, but drunk, I couldn't keep up, it was embarrassing. A middle-aged woman versus a young man in his prime, and she'd eaten me alive. It would never happen again. Slowly Ava roused. She shook her head and groaned.

'Oh God I feel terrible.'

I didn't say anything and felt awkward, wanting to disappear. Stupid mewed. When it came to Stupid and her remarkable powers of speech Ava was one of the few doubters.

'What's she saying?'

'She wants to be fed.'

'You'd better take her home then.'

This was certainly a hint and as nobody likes to overstay a welcome…

'I think I'll do the off.'

Ava turned to me.

'You're okay about this yeah?'

Was I okay about it? I thought I was. I nodded.

'Be sure to keep it to yourself then or otherwise.'

This comment freaked me, but I knew exactly where Ava was coming from. I jumped into my clothes and picked up Stupid.

'Bye Ave.'

'Bye Joseph.

7

It was late Friday afternoon and me and Ronnie were sitting in the front room of the flat, drinking a cold beer each, and ruminating on how we could ever get our hands on enough bees and honey to make our Mexican adventure a reality. At present the trip was as likely to happen as one of us walking on the moon. Ronnie took a reflective sip of beer and leaned back in his chair.

'I've been thinking.'

'You don't wanna be doing that, might strain something.'

'Shut up. Listen, if we sell all our electronic crap it should be enough to cover airfare to the land of the sombrero.'

'And why would we do that? We can't fly to Mexico without money.'

'We'll get open tickets. This will motivate us; make sure we don't get side-tracked. Once we've got the tickets all we need is spending money.'

'By selling all our electronic crap as you put it, does that also include our indispensable, can't live without it, laptop?'

'The laptops go, everything goes, even our mobile phones. I, like the rest of the fucking world, am suffering from an acute case of technology fatigue. And where we'll be going we won't be needing any of that shit anyway.'

Technology fatigue? I thought about the laptop, my gateway to the internet and all things online, without which I would be disconnected. 'Are you sure about the laptop?'

Ronnie nodded. 'Superfluous shit we no longer have a use for and like I say, we need all the bees and honey we can get our hands on.'

Put like that, the laptop had to be jettisoned. Now I was excited. Nothing was going to stop us getting to Mexico. 'Yeah, fuck it, onwards and upwards, and by any means necessary. Modern life is rubbish anyway.'

'Fucking right. Most of the technology we use has been put in place by the powers that be and the money makers to monitor our every move. Well fuck them - I'm going incognito.'

'Incognito?'

'Disappearing off the face of the fucking earth.'

'Not without me you're not.'

'That's right. And anyway I've still got a few tricks up my sleeve in regards to our current financial predicament. Never, ever give up, no fucking surrender, remember we're doing this for keeps!'

That evening we found ourselves in the Flower Pot. Everyone was there. It started out as just another Friday night piss-up. Ronnie and I plotted at the bar and listened to the fractured convos going on all around, the typical bullshit lies and delusions of grandeur.

Tony Baloney was holding court, acting like the Godfather or Gordon Gecko, but despite all his bullshit and dodgy ways, Baloney possessed something most people lack, charisma and star quality. If he hadn't decided to be a gangster he could've been anything he wanted to be.

At ten Angel walked in with a gang of mates. They were loud, obvious, and glamorous. I avoided eye contact and was glad she didn't come over and stand next to Baloney, an awkward scene I was keen to avoid. Deep down I still fancied Angel and more than once regretted ending the relationship. Tonight, with the war paint on and dressed to turn heads, she looked especially captivating. Once more I wondered if I had a brain malfunction, a peculiar form of dementedness or that I was basically an idiot.

I eyeballed Baloney. Okay he was loaded, drove a flash

car and drew respect from all and sundry, but at heart he was a sadistic and evil bastard. What the fuck was Angel thinking?

The evening flew by and as soon as the bugle appeared on the scene we were out for the duration. After that it was drinks at the bar, trips to the toilet, and vice versa. DJ Twisted Wheel played a decent selection of oldies and got everyone in the groove. It was Northern Soul mostly and when he dropped Bobby Relf's *Blowing My Mind to Pieces*, the place started jumping. The teenyboppers strutted their stuff on the dance floor. Girls pulled shapes like they were supermodels on a Milan catwalk, and the geezers did a good impression of John Travolta on speed. It was early days, but already the evening was imbued with that special Friday night edge. It was the start of the weekend.

Baloney and Ronnie disappeared and I was left standing at the bar, alone. Angel shimmied over.

'Norman no mates are we?'

'Just the way I like it.'

Angel downed the rest of her drink and glanced from the empty glass to the bar. I shrugged my shoulders.

'What d'ya want?'

Angel shuffled closer.

'The usual.'

'What's that then?' I said with a grin.

'Ha, ha, very funny.'

I tried summoning the attention of one of the bar staff or Alfie the landlord.

'Still shagging salami?'

'You'd better not let him hear you say that.'

'What's he gonna do, shoot me?'

Angel flicked some of her fringe away from her eyes and bit the bottom of her lower lip, like she always did when flirting.

'Anyways, I only saw him couple of times, it was over weeks ago.'

'Another notch on the bedpost of the sausage man,' I mumbled.

'What did you say?'

'Nothing.'

'So, still in the market for grannies are we?'

'What?'

Angel placed one hand on her hip and smiled a victory smile.

'Pearl's Café mean anything?'

I turned to the bar.

'Unbelievable,' I said over my shoulder

Once served I handed Angel a double vodka and cranberry juice.

'So, what you up to tonight?'

Angel sucked some of the liquid through a black straw and bopped her head in time to *Get Ready* by The Temptations.

'Donna's parents are on holiday so she's having an impromptu party round hers, you an Ronnie can come if ya want?'

'Really?'

'Yeah, really sad boy, but if you do decide to make an appearance, be sure to bring plenty of good foot.'

'Ha, knew they'd be catch.'

'Whatever.'

8

By the time we pulled into the drive of Donna's parents spacious five bedroom detached house the party was in full flow and the place was rocking. DJ Twisted Wheel had relocated from the Flower Pot and the smoke filled rooms were packed with bodies getting down to it as the Wheel pumped out classic sixties garage. When the unmistakable sound of *Louie Louie* by the Kingsmen blasted out everyone went crazy.

We bumped into Baby Donna and Angel in the kitchen. After snorting a long line of coke Baby Donna eyed us.

'Hey, the secret squirrels are here, how goes it boys?'

'Secret what?' said Ronnie, as he chopped out some lines.

Baby Donna stood up and dabbed the end of her petite upturned nose.

'Don't worry, your secret's safe with us.'

Ronnie rolled a fifty pound note, lowered his head to the work surface, and stuck one end of the note into his nostril. He looked at Baby Donna sideways.

'It'd better be.'

Baby Donna laughed and cocked her head to one side.

'Tune,' she said, before marching off into the living room, taking Angel with her.

'Alright?' I said, as Angel squeezed past.

'Meet me later.'

The night flew by in a drunken and drugged haze. I found myself in the garden, taking a lengthy eyelash into a huge potted plant, when I was rudely interrupted mid-flow.

'Oh God, can't you make it to the toilet?'

I glanced over my shoulder. It was Angel.

'Wanna hold it?'

'Get fucked.'

I shook dry. 'Love to, any offers?'

My ex stood there in the shadows, one hand holding a cigarette, the other a large drink.

'How could any classy girl turn down such an inviting offer?'

'What about a quick tongue session?'

It was then that Angel came close, very, very close.

'Meet me in the bathroom,' she breathed lustily, kissing me full on the lips.

'What bathroom? There are four of the fuckers.'

Angel walked away.

'The one in the loft conversion.'

'When?'

'Five minutes.'

'Five minutes?'

Angel stuck out an outstretched hand, fingers and thumb wiggling.

Five minutes later I was outside a closed bathroom door wondering what the fuck I was doing. No revellers had ventured that far up the house and I was all alone. The coke paranoia hit me. Was Angel inside, was it a wind-up, was someone filming me loitering outside like a complete plank? Anything was possible.

I took another hit of beer and tried the handle. It was locked. Shit. I pressed my ear against the door, total silence. Then the door flung open and I fell inside.

'Sssh,' whispered Angel.

I picked myself up. Angel was wearing a silk dressing gown and holding a bottle of champagne.

'What the fuck's going on?'

In the corner of the room a Jacuzzi bubbled away, steam clouds rising attractively. Angel locked the bathroom door and loosened her gown. I watched transfixed as she stepped out of that gown, revealing thighs, derriere, curvature of the spine. As she ascended the steps of the jacuzzi, she looked like a silent movie star before disappearing into the bubbles.

'What ya gonna do, stand there all night?' the re-incarnation of Louise Brooks said.

I put my beer to one side and stripped off. As soon as I hit the bubbles Angel jumped me.

'I thought we'd split-up?'

'We have and you won't be getting any more, so make the most of it.'

Afterwards, as we lay in the afterglow of druggy drunken sex, I did what all men do in these situations and began bullshitting.

'I love you, why don't we go to Las Vegas and get married by an Elvis impersonator?'

Angel lit another cigarette and gave me a swift dig in the left kidney, a rabbit punch.

'You just don't get it do ya?'

'Get what?' I wheezed.

'Me and you are yesterday, finito. You well and truly blew it.'

'Didn't seem that way five minutes ago.'

Angel blew some smoke in my face and sipped champagne.

'I only did that because I felt horny and you were available, it's unlikely to ever happen again in either of our lifetimes.'

I wafted the smoke from my visage and grabbed my champagne glass.

'Ah well, at least we went out on a high.'

Angel sighed dreamily. 'Yeah, even though you're a complete idiot that was one hot mother-fucking shag.'

Just as I was wondering whether that was a compliment or not the bathroom door handle rattled several times.

'Who the fuck is that?'

Angel raised a finger to her lips.

'Shuussh, whoever it is they'll go away eventually.'

We sat there in the tub, looking at each other. Seconds later there was a loud rap on the door.

'Who the fuck's in there?'

'Who the fuck wants to know?'

'Me, Stuart.'

Angel and I shot each other 'oh no' stares. Eyes Down.

'Fuck off Eyes Down,' I called out.

This was followed by more door banging.

'What the fuck? Who the fuck called me Eyes Down? Is that you in there Ridgwell? I'll fucking get ya when ya come out geezer, keep looking over ya shoulder.'

I went to fire another barbed retort, but Angel clamped a hand over my mouth, hard. Moments later we heard footsteps on the stairs, growing fainter. Angel took her hand away.

'That cunt's taking things beyond the limit,' I said.

Angel stepped out of the jacuzzi and slipped into her silk dressing gown.

'You wanna watch him.'

I lay back and relaxed in the bubbles.

'What d'ya mean?'

'He's a wrong un.'

'Fuck him.'

Angel opened the bathroom door.

'See ya downstairs sad boy.'

I turned the jacuzzi off and lay in the still, warm water.

Some spermatozoa floated on the bottom of the pool along with the odd pube. I swigged champagne from the bottle, blew-off, and watched as a string of jam tart bubbles rose to the surface like pearls.

-9-

When I got downstairs, the sun was rising in the east, a smudge of red throbbing through a window. Ronnie and Angel were nowhere to be seen, or Baby Donna for that matter. Unfortunately the first person I bumped into was Eyes Down, busy snorting coke from a kitchen work surface.

'Stuart, seen Ronnie?'

Eyes Down looked up, clocked me, and rushed over until he was right in my face. Sweat was popping out all over his head and his boat was bright red.

'Think ya fucking funny, cunt?'

Surprised by this act of aggression, I backed off.

'Take it easy geez.'

Eyes Down followed up once more until he was right in my fucking face again. A huge coke bogie dangled from one of his reddened nostrils, a disgusting sight that nauseated me.

'Whaddya mean take it easy, why the fuck should I take if easy? Everyone thinks they can take the piss out of me, but I ain't standing for it no more. People should learn some fucking respect!'

Once again I backed off. Another good reason to get the fuck out of London. Mindless idiots like Eyes Down, whose idea of a good time was to snort as much coke as possible until they became delusional or wanted to kill someone.

'Yeah, totally with ya Stu, but where the fuck is everyone?'

Eyes Down chopped out lines of cocaine with a credit card.

'With me, with me, I don't want ya fucking with me.'

What a cunt, I thought. What a moody fucking cunt.

It was then that Surfer Boy appeared on the scene. His perma-tan had faded, but unlike Eyes Down he was in good spirits. I was relieved to see him, relieved for any kind of diversion from the increasingly unpredictable behaviour of a coked-up Stuart.

'Where the fuck ave you been?' said Surfer.

'Don't worry where I've been, where the fuck is everyone else?'

'All outside, the house party having now morphed into a pool party.'

'Quality.'

SB noticed Eyes Down for the first time.

'Alright Stu, what ya hiding in here for?'

Eyes Down leaned over and snorted another line.

'An you can fuck off an all.'

Surfer Boy shot me a stare as if to say what the fuck's wrong with him? I grabbed a cold one from the fridge, shrugged my shoulders and walked into the garden. It was all getting claustrophobic inside.

The remaining revelers were strung out around the outdoor pool like a fucked up gang of ghostly figurines. The pool itself contained no water, and persons unknown had rigged up a turntable and speakers inside and some tinny hardcore techno blasted out.

I saw Angel lying with a spaced-out geezer on a sunlounger. I'd never seen the guy before, but he looked like some defunct member of a long-forgotten boy band. I thought about the shag in the jacuzzi and smiled. Baby Donna lay draped across a redundant diving board, sunglasses on, tall drink in hand, looking powerful.

I spotted Ronnie involved in an in-depth convo with Tony Baloney and strolled over.

'Where the fuck ya been?' said Ronnie.

I wondered why everyone was worried about where I'd been.

'Nowhere.'

Baloney took a hit from a silver phial and handed it to me. I wasn't sure how it worked. Baloney clocked my hesitancy.

'Turn it to the right. How's Pearl?'

At the mention of Pearl's name a wave of anxiety hit me. Yet another reason to get the fuck out of London. Living in the same area all your life meant everyone knew your business. Then there were the parties and the drugs, especially the drugs. Whereas earlier everyone had been in party mood, now narcotic-induced tension and paranoia were everywhere or maybe it was me. Was it me? I handed back the phial and snorted until the coke dripped down the back of my throat, the best part of the buzz.

'Fucked if I know,' I sniffed.

Baloney smiled at that, but said nothing, his silence resonating like a curious itch.

I sipped my beer, buzzed nicely on the bugle, and thought about stuff. The party had started out great, but was now deteriorating into a messy drugged up bleary-eyed overkill. Maybe it was time to swerve. The thrill was gone, but maybe it had never been there in the first place. The remaining revellers were a little the worse for wear. A couple of people danced inside the pool or rather staggered around, eyes glazed, brains squashed. Did I really want to be doing this anymore? Was this really all life had to offer a young man? As these future thoughts flitted through my addled mind Baby Donna slithered away from the diving board and strolled over to Baloney. After a whispered convo Baloney stood up and made a declaration.

'Party's over, come on suckers Royal Oak's our next destination, place starts to rock around this time.'

Immediately everyone was up for it. Well, everyone who was left that is, Ronnie, Angel, Baby Donna, Surfer Boy and yours truly all piling into Baloney's convertible Volkswagen GTi. The last person to find a place in a car, predictably, was Eyes Down. He shuffled over to Baloney's Volks.

'Got room for one more?' he asked timidly.

Baloney turned the key in the ignition of the high-powered Volks and revved the engine, loud.

'On your own.'

'What?'

'In ya own time.'

Then we were gone, Eyes Down left standing on the gravelled drive like a jilted groom.

10

Tony Baloney drove like a crazed person. High on drink and coke the inner city roads became a Formula 1 racetrack. The roof of the Volks was down; Angel and Baby Donna were nestled safely in the back seat, while me and Surfer Boy were on the ledge above, one hand holding tight to the middle intersection, the other clenching a can of wife beater.

Ronnie fiddled with the sound system.

'How the fuck does this shit work?'

'Fuck, take it easy Tone,' I yelled, as Baloney took a corner at over fifty miles an hour and my beer went flying. Baloney hit the accelerator and Ronnie hit the on button.

'What are ya, a man or a mouse?' roared Baloney.

If anything, with the sounds blasting, Baloney drove even faster. Angel and Baby Donna held each other tight and screamed. Baloney wasn't listening, his face etched with concentration, totally focused. In fact, despite his advanced state of intoxication, he appeared to be in what sports psychologists often refer to as, The Zone.

Everything, houses, cars, shops and people, flashed by in a crazy blur. Ronnie and Surfer Boy waved their hands in the air and the girls continued screaming. I was holding on tight, yet enjoying the death drive, safe in the knowledge that I wasn't going to die because my ultimate destiny was Mexico.

Baloney approached the next corner at supersonic rates. Everyone in the car screamed, even Ronnie.

This is it I thought. I will NEVER get to Mexico.

The wheels screeched, burning rubber filled the air, and a shadow flashed before my eyes. After mastering the corner Baloney let out a whoop of delight and the girls started crying, but a hundred yards down the road I realised Surfer Boy was no longer inside the vehicle.

'STOP THE FUCKING CAR!'

Angel and Baby Donna looked up, frightened eyes darting around. Baloney glanced over his shoulder.

'What?'

'Surfer Boy.'

'Surfer Boy?'

'He's not in the fucking car.'

Without another word Baloney executed a high-speed u-turn. There was more screeching wheels, burning rubber, more screams. Five seconds later we were back at the corner where Surfer Boy had disappeared. We found him sitting on a patch of grass, blood pouring from a head wound, but amazingly still holding his beer can.

On clocking us he raised the can.

'Oi, Oi, Oi.'

'Quick, get him in the motor,' growled Baloney.

Me and Ronnie jumped out of the car and bundled Surfer Boy into the back of the Volks. The girls tended to SB's wounds, while Ronnie and Baloney had a very vocal argument.

'Who the fuck d'ya think ya are, James fucking Hunt?' raged Ronnie.

'Fuck off,' responded Baloney drily.

'What d'ya mean fuck off? You could've killed Surfer Boy, now just slow down for fucksakes.'

'Fuck off.'

Once the claret was wiped away Surfer Boy's head wound was superficial, and aside from a few cuts and grazes he was otherwise intact. The only concern was that he was talking nonsense.

'You okay Surf?'

'Bubba, shumba, sunshine reggae, Charlie spliff.'

Angel shook her head sadly.

'He's lost it.'

Ronnie leaned over.

'He's alright. Just got a little concussion.'

'Shouldn't we take him to hospital?'

'Dunno, let's ask the mug. Surfs d'ya wanna go Ospital?'

A blessed-out look adorned SB's visage.

'Na, fucky, fucky, fancy a game of pool?'

Despite the gravity of the situation, we all burst out laughing.

By the time we got to the Royal Oak the Flower Market was up and running, the crowds already out for a leisurely Sunday morning browse amongst the bouquets and bric-a-brac shops. Inside the run-down boozer it was a different story. The interior was like a crack-den. Loud rock music blasting, freaks for bar staff, and ten or twenty hipsters dancing in a dirty back room to old 1980's pop hits. As for the rest of the clientele they were as drugged up as it is possible to be without overdosing. The Royal Oak had once been a traditional boozer, but like the rest of Shoreditch and Hoxton had been overrun by trendies, scenesters and assorted freaks from all over the globe.

After getting a round of drinks for everyone Baloney produced a plastic bag containing a quantity of yellow pills.

'Pills anyone?' he offered breezily.

Everyone dipped their hand inside, except me.

'What are they?' I asked.

Baloney smiled a sickly smile.

'Yellow Calis.'

I dipped my hand in and grabbed a couple.

'What like the ones from 89?'

Baloney rested a hand on my shoulder.

'Better than the ones from 89.'

It was impossible for me to believe the veracity of this statement. Anyone who knew anything about the production of ecstasy knew the 1989 batch of Yellow Californians had never been surpassed, attaining legendary status amongst those in the know.

'I'll believe that when I feel the rushes.'

'Oh you're feel the rushes alright. In fact I wouldn't take a whole as they are proper powerful, a whole could tip you over.'

Unfortunately I'd just double-dropped and this offhand comment filled me with acute anxiety.

11

As soon as the effects of the Yellow Calis kicked in a rapid descent into the murky world of lost-it narcotic freakiness was the reward. Wandering the pub on my own, it was difficult to focus or walk in a straight line. I hallucinated. People's faces fell apart, digital images appeared out of nowhere, and sounds echoed and reverberated discordantly.

I swayed to the bar, grasped the rail for support, sweat pouring from me in rivers. Gripped by an intense paranoia I took deep breaths. Then I spotted Ronnie. He was sitting on a leather settee, surrounded by five or six pretty girls Hugh Heffner style. I wondered how he did it. I caught his attention and waved him over. He made excuses. The girls smiled happily.

'You okay?' he asked.

Another powerful body rush hit me.

'Whoa, yeah, those pills almost knocked me out the game.'

'Get a pint to counter the effects. In fact get me one as well.'

I ordered a couple of pints of Stella from a sophisticated barmaid who might've been a catwalk model but for her eyes, which were too close together. When the pints came I took a huge swig.

'Who are the girls?'

'Bunch of art students, buzzing out on speed, know fuck all about art.'

I was glad for the conversation. It gave me something else to think about, breathing space from the extra-sensory narcotic overload, but it took all my powers of concentration to keep it going.

'Whaddya mean?'

'Still talking about Warhol and De Kooning, even Pollock and Brit Art. I blame the lecturers, clueless fucks mostly.'

This was good, a typical Ronnie conversation, which in turn meant I was not completely twisted.

'What did you say?'

'I gave it to em, told em modern art had crawled up a dead end. Told em it was defunct.'

I felt another powerful body rush, it was a fucking strong one. I licked my lips and gurned involuntarily.

'Still a good deal of money to be made from it though, if you're successful I mean.'

'That doesn't make it great art, it's mostly instantly forgettable art, and ultimately worthless.'

'But one of those girls might make it, shit all they need is a wealthy benefactor to come along and buy their stuff.'

'That's undoubtedly true, but it's a motherfucking lottery. Ninety-nine percent of these wannabe's artistic output is doomed to clog up someone's basement, and more than likely their own.'

I cocked an eyebrow and let out another involuntary gurn.

'Give em any other illuminations?'

'Yeah, I did, told em I was an artist as well and that I'd just invented a new genre.'

'A new genre?'

'Cosmic Realism, man.'

'Cosmic Realism, what the fuck's that?'

'The ability to conjure up an image so far-fetched and bizarre and obviously not based in any sort of reality, but which the viewer willingly accepts as the gospel truth.'

'And what did they think of that?'

'I don't think they were able to grasp the magnitude of what I was saying, you know it twisted their melons - went over their heads.'

'It's going over my head.'

'Mind you the ginger one was impressed. Even if she didn't understand a word, reckon I'll get me nuts in if I play my cards right.'

'You'll be lucky.'

Ronnie sauntered back to the art students. Shit, even my best mate looked strange. He was wearing the clothes of an eighteenth century dandy. I blinked. Now, he appeared to be in some 1970's get up. I closed my eyes and concentrated. The hallucinations were freaky yet fascinating at the same time. I opened my eyes, a man with a woman's body walked by. This was all getting too much.

I wandered into a back room. Angel and Baby Donna were in the middle of the dance floor, embracing and kissing the fuck out of each other. Shit, the old lesbian act again, although this time they were really getting into it, eyes closed, tonguing slowly and sensuously. Probably down to the Calis, I ruminated.

As I floated past I tapped Baby Donna on the shoulder.

'Can I join in?'

Baby Donna stopped kissing Angel and gave me a good, long slow one.

'Take it easy lover boy,' she whispered lustily, before Angel grabbed her by the head and resumed the tongues business. Angel didn't acknowledge me in any way. I staggered off into the darkness.

I found Surfer Boy sat in a neglected corner with his head in his hands. Someone had managed to get him a coffee, but he was still talking gibberish.

'Yo, Darren wass up?' I asked, using his real name for once.

Surfer looked at me out of glazed eyes.

'Fire engines, jumping, jumping.'

Shit, maybe he had lost it? I mean, what if he never got it

back, doomed to spend the rest of his life as a simpleton? This freaky thought made me shudder.

'Surf, it's me Ridgwell, you know your old mate Joe.'

Darren put an arm around my shoulder. 'Man, you're really out of it ain't ya?'

I glanced from side to side. Fuck, maybe it was me who had lost it?

As I fought furiously to contain the mad rushes, clinging tenuously to any notion of reality, the gates of hell opened and an evil atmosphere appeared on the scene. The dancers became aggressive and it wasn't long before the malevolent atmosphere enveloped the entire boozer. Paranoia struck deep, bad medicine in the house, a dodgy batch of pills and everyone on the same drug. My heart sank. Yellow Calis, Yellow fucking Calis! Where the fuck was Balony, the piss-taking cunt? Then Eyes Down appeared out of nowhere. His face red, flared nostrils blocked with coke bogies, a grotesque sight. Red spells danger.

'Get us a fucking drink,' he fired at me, his voice loaded with aggression.

Instantly the situation was fraught with peril. And to think, this was one of my alleged friends.

'What?'

'Get us a fucking drink, cunt!'

'What ya talking to me like that for?'

Eyes Down rushed over and pushed me against the wall. 'You wan it, I'm switching, I'm switching.'

His hot manky breath scorched my cheek. He made me feel sick. I pushed him away. No wonder everyone averted their gaze every time he showed his moody boat.

'Fuck off.'

Eyes Down shot out an arm and grabbed me by the throat. The swift movement took me by surprise, the air squeezed out of me. It became difficult to breathe, impossible to talk. Eyes Down looked like a maniac and for the first time I felt real fear. This nutter was actually trying to kill me. I fought frantically for breath.

'Eyes Down!'

The death grip on my throat relaxed as Ronnie's fist crashed into Stuart's face. Air rushed back into my lungs, and I choked and spluttered as Ronnie and Eyes Down wrestled across the wooden floor while everyone else shrieked and shouted. I followed as they tumbled out the back of the boozer. Everything was misty, blurred and nothing made sense. Bad vibrations. Keep it real, keep it real, keep it fucking real. I couldn't believe it, what the fuck was going on? I jumped between Ronnie and Eyes Down.

'What the fuck we doing, fighting each other?'

'You wanna ask this prick ere,' said Ronnie.

I felt a dull blow to the middle of my back. Eyes Down pushed me aside and ran off. Seconds later the cry went up from Baloney.

'Chiv! He's got a fucking chiv!'

I gave chase, stumbling behind Ronnie and Baloney as Eyes Down ran into a dead end. He turned around, slowly until he was facing us. I saw the blade in his hand, the silver glinting malevolently in the noon sunshine. Something warm trickled down my back. I stuck a hand inside my tee-shirt and felt liquid. When I withdrew my hand it was covered in red. I looked up.

'The cunt's chibbed me!'

Ronnie didn't hesitate. A flashing left crashed into Eyes Down's jaw with a crack. The knife fell from his hand and he dropped to the floor with a groan. Baloney followed up with the boot. My vision blurred and then I was falling, falling, falling...

-12-

I awoke in a darkened room, in a strange bed. Where the fuck was I? Somebody was holding my hand, a young Indian lady dressed in a nurse's uniform. The lady was smiling and immediately I liked her.

A needle and some tubing were attached to my left arm. The tubing led to a saline drip. From somewhere the beep of an electric monitor sounded. I was in hospital. What the fuck was I doing in hospital? My mouth was dry, and as well as an intense pain in my back, my head hurt.

Random events re-inserted themselves into my consciousness. I recalled Baby Donna's house party, shagging Angel in the jacuzzi, Surfer Boy falling out of the car, The Royal Oak, a fight, something bad happening, but what? As sketchy details of another long lost weekend filtered through the steel wires of my brain, the nurse addressed me directly.

'How are you?'

She had big brown eyes, filled with kindness and compassion. I felt an over-whelming urge to kiss her. The nurse produced a thermometer and plumped it into my mouth.

'What happened to me?'

The nurse felt my brow.

'You don't remember?'

I shook my head.

'You're very lucky.'

'I am?'

'Yes, now go back to sleep, you must rest.'

'But what did happen to me?'

The nurse smiled tenderly. 'I prayed for you last night and my prayers were answered. Now go to sleep, I insist.'

A wave of sweet fragrance hit me, a perfume and then the nurse was gone, soft footsteps padding along the ward. I lay there in the dark and felt very tired. I closed my eyes and fell into a deep sleep.

When I awoke I found myself in a ward filled with old men, most of whom looked dead or about to die. The expansive room was bathed in bright sunlight, forcing me to squint. I studied those old men carefully. Why had I been put in with all the oldies? I was still unable to recall what had happened, but figured it was some sort of drugs overdose. I vowed then and there to quit drugs and stick to beer.

A short while later I was served breakfast. Well, they called it breakfast, but the food was inedible. I shoved the tray aside, untouched. A bevy of doctors appeared and surrounded my bed. Someone drew the curtains. With all those eyes trained on me I felt special. One Doctor, the leader, faced me.

'How are you feeling today Joseph?'

'Not too bad.'

'You've had quite a traumatic experience, haven't you?'

'Ave I?'

'Yes, you were stabbed in the back by a known assailant. We are keeping you in for observation.'

Stabbed? A snapshot flashed before my eyes. Eyes Down, a knife glinting malevolently in the morning light, a weapon held in the hand of an alleged friend. He had stabbed me in the back, the cowardly dog. I lay there freaking, ruminating on the fact that my life had nearly been taken away from me, as medical mutterings filled the air. Then the leader Doc turned to the junior docs and spoke about me in the third person.

'The wound is located on the left side of the back, 22 inches below the top of the head and 2 inches from the front of the body. After approximation of the edges it measures one and a half inches in length and is diagonally oriented; the posterior aspect is dull or flat, measuring one and a half inches and the anterior aspect is pointed or tapered. Possible lung puncture...'

It was pure physician babble and understanding only a few words, I closed my eyes and drifted off again. To a foreign land, a sun-kissed beach, swaying palms, beautiful senoritas, the sound of gentle mambo playing in soft southern winds...

-13-

When I re-opened my eyes the bevy of doctors had been replaced by Angel and Baby Donna, aesthetically speaking, a more pleasing sight than the quacks. Angel squeezed my hand.

'How ya feeling?'

Aside from the dull ache in my back I was feeling fine and now, being a man of good fortune and born under a lucky star, I decided to milk the situation.

'Terrible, got a punctured lung, Doc says I might not make it.'

Angel and Bay Donna's eyes opened wide with horror.

'Really, we didn't think it was that bad, the nurses said you were doing better than expected.'

'And to think, it was Eyes Down who tried to kill me,' I added with a whimper.

Angel's face darkened.

'Yeah, well, that prick ain't doing too well either.'

'How comes?'

'Balony and Ronnie kicked the shit out of him.'

Angel reeled off Eyes Down's injuries. 'Fractured jaw, six broken ribs, broken hand. I still don't know what the sad fuck was thinking.'

This news, although gruesome, cheered me.

'At least that's something.'

Baby Donna leaned over and whispered in my ear.

'My Old Man said he'll put out a contract on him if ya like.'

I contemplated a hit man taking out Eyes Down with a bullet to the head and disposing of the evidence in the murky depths of the River Thames, the body weighed down with lumps of concrete. Again, the gruesome images cheered me.

'That scenario will only be necessary if I don't pull through.'

Then I paused for effect before letting out an agonised groan.

Angel leapt to my side.

'Are you okay, is there anything we can do?'

'Shall we call a nurse over?' asked Baby Donna, her little girl voice filled with genuine concern.

'There is one thing you could do,' I replied croakily.

'What's that?'

I glanced towards my midriff.

'A Bombay Roll wouldn't go amiss.'

At that the girls jumped back, all concern evaporating in an instant.

'You what?'

'Might help alleviate the pain, ooh, it's really bad.'

'You cheeky fucker, there's us thinking you're at death's door,' said Angel.

'Well I am, sort of.'

'You haven't changed ave ya? Almost get laid down an still only thinking of one thing.'

Baby Donna pulled the curtain around my bed with a resounding swish.

'I know, why don't we go one better?' she said to Angel.

'You mean?'

'Yeah, I mean rape the invalid, in his condition I don't think he'll put up much resistance.'

'Ha, ha very funny Baby,' I said nervously.

The two girls approached the bed. I pulled the bed sheet tight around my chin. A tit-ride was one thing, but getting jumped by too horny bitches filled me with terror.

'Take it easy ladies, I'll scream!'

Angel and Baby Donna recoiled in disgust.

'Come on let's go. Obviously not gonna get any action round here with this homo,' said Baby Donna.

I breathed a sigh of relief.

'Bye girls, thanks for coming.'

'Bye Jo-Jo.'

Moments later Ronnie appeared on the scene. Despite the stultifying temperature of the ward his leather jacket was zipped all the way up to the neck, and he was walking in a strange jerky manner. Plus he was talking to himself.

'Oi, no, ah, eek, easy, sort it out.'

I propped myself up in bed. Ronnie pulled the curtain around my bed and sat down gingerly. He fidgeted in his chair, holding his arms across his stomach.

'You okay?'

Ronnie jerked sharply to the left. 'Fuck that hurt.'

'What the fuck's that matter with ya?'

I heard a few strangulated word-like meows, and my heart roared. Ronnie unzipped his leather jacket.

'Oh fuck, can't hide her any longer.'

'Stupid,' I cried out in delight.

Ronnie held a finger to his lips.

'Shussh, we'll get chucked out.'

I calmed in an instant. Stupid jumped onto the bed, eyeballed me, sniffed the air, and climbed on top of my head. Seconds later I lay there like some weird invalided Cossack while Ronnie got straight down to business.

'First things first. You don't have to worry about Eyes Down. He's been taken care of.'

'Yeah, I know, Angel and Baby Donna told me.'

'Really? Well good. And you won't have to see him again. He's barred from London.'

'Barred from London?'

'For life. Second thing, as soon as you're well enough we're going to Mexico.

I've sorted out our tickets and even our visas for Australia, which will be the next onward step in our world trip.'

'Our world trip, Australia? What about monies?'

'All taken care of.'

'How?'

'Don't worry about how; just make sure ya get fit. I'll explain everything when ya get home. What did the docs say?'

'No worries, the cut's only superficial. They're keeping me in for observation, standard procedure.'

'Good.'

After this we talked about the night of the stabbing, going over all the messy details, dissecting events, analysing motives, but it didn't change the fact that I'd nearly become another grim statistic, another young victim of modern big city life.

'Just one more compelling reason to get the fuck out of the country,' said Ronnie.

I raised one arm and softly stroked Stupid's nose until she purred contentedly.

'It's weird. It's like fate is conspiring against us at every opportunity, I mean I'm beginning to think we'll never get there.'

'I don't wanna hear any of that bullshit.'

'What bullshit?'

'Negative vibes.'

'I'm just saying.'

'Well don't. We gonna get there, no matter what it takes and with cunts like Eyes Down around I can't fucking wait.'

'You don't think he'll show his face for a while do ya?'

'Na, but he's a wrong un an ya can never trust a wrong-un, ever.'

'You can say that again.'

Ronnie picked Stupid up and, despite several protest meows, shoved her back inside his jacket.

'Right gotta go, gives us a bell when ya get discharged and I'll come an pick you up.'

'Watch it,' I whispered, as a Nurse appeared at the curtain.

Ronnie bobbed and weaved and grimaced. The mews kept coming so he spoke in a very loud voice.

'See ya later man.'

-14-

Two days later I was out of hospital and back at home, feet up, swigging beer like nothing had happened. Had I cheated death? Maybe, maybe not. Life was a lottery, a game of chance, one day alive, the next day dead. And if it could happen to me, it could happen to you; in fact it could happen to anyone.

The stabbing reminded me of my own mortality and human frailty, making me determined to get the most out of whatever time was left. I wasn't going to piss it away in a job I didn't like, performing pointless tasks, surrounded by strange turds I had zero in common with. I was going to see the world, embark on crazy adventures and live life at full-throttle. There would be no time for regrets.

Despite these grandiose proclamations the perennial problem remained - a desperate lack of money. Shit, the stuff was only made out of paper, so why was I unable to get my hands on any? I lacked financial acumen, the ability to turn a penny into a pound, and the prospect of hard work made me baulk. Was I lazy, a born idler, someone who would never amount to anything in the world? I wasn't convinced. I could work as hard as the next person, but lacked motivation and ambition. Doing the same thing over and over seemed pointless, a waste of precious time and in the final analysis, inexcusable. That was existence and I wanted to live.

Money, money, money. The root of all evil, the bane of man's existence, but without it life was a dull affair that reduced the day-to-day living to a desperate scramble for survival. The words of William Blake dominated my every waking thought. 'I must create my own system or be enslaved by another man's!' But that was alright for old Blakey to say.

He wasn't living on a sink estate in a deprived area of East London, recovering from a near fatal stab wound. And anyway he was long dead.

Then there was Ronnie. We were going to Mexico, he said. Had it all planned and sorted, he said. He would explain everything once I got out of the hospital, he said. Well, I was out and he hadn't mentioned a fucking thing, and whenever I broached the subject he acted mysterious. He was evasive. Then he kept disappearing. Fuck it, he was like the Scarlet Pimpernel.

-15-

A day later Ronnie revealed his plan and boy was I in for a shock. I was lounging on the settee, re-reading *Tristessa* by Jack Kerouac, and dreaming of Mexico City when Ronnie returned from one of his mystery trips and gave me the low down.

'Next Wednesday we do a little job and the following evening fly to Mexico. If everything goes according to plan we'll have fifty thou. Twenty-five each. That'll do us for at least a year or two until we go to Australia and find work. After that we play it by ear.'

I liked the sound of twenty-five grand each, but I didn't like the sound of next Wednesday we do a little job. I didn't like the sound of that at all. I zapped the television off with the remote control.

'We do a little job?'

'Bank job.'

'What the fuck?'

'Building society to be precise, inside job, straight in, straight out.'

'What the fuck?'

'I do the stick-up, you're the getaway driver. Like I say, straight in straight out, won't even use a mother-fucking gun.'

'And the punch line?'

Ronnie said nothing. Had my friend lost his mind?

'Are you serious?'

'I'm deadly serious.'

Once I'd recovered some sort of equilibrium, I got Ronnie to explain everything. He was indeed deadly serious about robbing a High Street building society. And once we'd been over the details the idea became plausible, even desirable. Pound signs flashed before my eyes, easy money, avarice, greed, stupidity. I'd drive Ronnie to the building society. Just before opening, several local wholesalers deposited a week's takings mid-week, every week. The place would be over flowing with cash.

'And if we get caught?'

'Unarmed and our first offence, we might escape with probation.'

'Probation?'

'Why not? I'm gonna rob the place with an imitation piece and if I get caught claim insanity.'

'And what will I claim?'

'Misplaced loyalty to your dear old mate.'

'Nice.'

'Listen, it's the ideal time to rob a bank.'

'That's debatable.'

'Check the figures. Despite what the media might say, since the turn of the century actual bank robberies have been in decline.'

'And the reason?'

'Tightened security, but mostly criminals adopting less traditional crime methods.'

'Tightened security?'

'Which has led to complacency amongst banks and bank staff, they just don't expect to get robbed these days. Anyway all the money's insured. Staff are instructed to hand the shit over. The banks reclaim the losses and pass any costs incurred onto their easily subjugated customers.'

I tried to take everything in. Ronnie had always been a dreamer; someone prepared to do things a little differently from the crowd. It was why I'd been so attracted to him in the first place, from the very first day I met him in our local library, that and our shared love of literature. Fuck, aged ten he'd walked into his nearest Roman Catholic Church and stated his burning desire to become a priest. He just wanted to know about everything he once told me, how trees grew, why the sky was blue, even the secrets of the cosmos. And the books we devoured opened up brand new worlds of untold adventure and excitement, filled with crazy characters living life at full throttle, people going places and doing things, madcap seers seeking truth in an unknowable universe. And now this latest idea to get out of the rat race, to drop out of society and follow the road, a bank job. It was a one-way ticket to a lengthy spell of bird and lime.

'I've got a better idea,' I said.

'What's that?'

'Why don't we get proper jobs and save money from our salaries like normal people?'

Ronnie was mortified. He checked himself all over and eyeballed me.

'Do I look like a normal person?'

'Now ya come to mention it.'

'And you're the epitome of un-normal, but let me allay any fears you may possess.'

'Yes do, for I'm not just fearful, I'm completely terrified.'

With that Ronnie outlined the job in microscopic detail. He covered preparation, back-up plans, location, timings, lines of communication and sources of information. He made robbing a bank sound as easy as taking candy from a baby, which it wasn't because if it was everyone would be at it.

'But ultimately,' declared Ronnie emphatically, 'in the final analysis, if by some freak occurrence something does go wrong I'm man enough to face the consequences.'

I remained silent for a few moments, ruminating on the fact that my life was either about to enter a new dynamic phase of unlimited excitement or about to unravel right before my very eyes.

'My fears have in no way been allayed.'

'Think about it. You could be dead, and what ave we done? There's a big wide world out there and I want to see it. One-off bank robbers rarely get caught. Bank robbers get caught because they can't resist robbing again. That's a mug's game. After this job we go legit.'

-16-

And then my beloved pet died. It happened in the wee small hours. After an eight hour booze session in the Pot I'd awoken with a great thirst. Stupid was not asleep on top of my head like usual. I stumbled out of bed and into the kitchen in search of re-hydration in the form of an ice cold drink. And there she was, stretched out on the linoleum struggling for breath, in fact in her death throes.

I cradled her in my arms. Instinctively I knew my pet was going to die. Stupid and I had grown up together and she was as much a part of my life as anyone, an integral cog in my lifecycle. I looked deep into her blue eyes. Stupid was eighteen, a great age for any feline. For the last couple of years she'd been suffering from an over-active thyroid gland, and that debilitating condition combined with her many fractures, meant it was only a matter of time.

Stupid emitted a series of rasping wheezes. I stroked her nose and tickled her under the chin. The painful wheezes continued unabated, agonising and unrelenting. She was slipping away, the light of life fading from her beautiful blue eyes. I cradled her in my arms and whispered words of love. Eventually the sun rose in the east and it was all over.

Almost immediately Stupid's body stiffened from the effects of rigor mortis. I put her down and woke Ronnie.

'What's up?'

'Stupid's dead.'

'Fuck.'

'I'm going to bury her under the weeping willow in the garden. Could ya give us a hand?'

'Of course I fucking can.'

Half an hour later, with the help of a garden spade, the grave was dug. I even fashioned a wooden cross to mark the resting place. As I lowered Stupid into the pit, the leaves of the weeping willow rustled and a songbird let go with a tremulous crescendo of sweet notes. I said a quick prayer to the God of all things and the service was over. On the cross were carved these words:

Stupid (Buried with all her Magic) R.I.P

Ronnie placed a hand on my shoulder.

'You alright geez?'

'Yeah, yeah, I just want a few moments by myself.'

Once alone I knelt by the edge of the grave and thought about stuff. I thought about the bank job. A crazy idea, reckless, even suicidal, but I had to get away. All things must pass. Start afresh, a clean slate, and commence another chapter in life. There was nothing for me in London. The passing of Stupid signified the end of an era. It was time to move on.

So far I hadn't cried, but when I walked into the kitchen and saw Stupid's orange twin bowl, one for water, one for meat, it choked me up. Death was strange. What happened to an animal or even a human after the final act had played out? Reincarnation? Anything was possible, but once the light of life went out, nothing else was there. I'd studied Stupid after she passed away and it wasn't her. There was no hint of her magical personality, no twinkle in her eye, just a dead cat of nothingness. The tears fell like stardust dreams...

-17-

On Tuesday morning there was a dramatic change of plan. Ronnie woke me in the middle of the night.

'Let's go, go, go!'

I shot straight up in bed.

'What the...'

Ronnie whipped my quilt off.

'I'll explain on the way, but we've just had one of those touches that only come round once in a blue moon, now let's fucking go.'

'So what the fuck are we doing?' I asked, as we drove along desolate and eerily deserted London streets in a stolen car.

'Goods lorry, can you drive a truck?'

I shook my head.

'Didn't think so, those air-breaks take some getting used to.'

Thirty minutes later we pulled into an ordinary suburban street in West London, just past Wembley. Ronnie handed me a pair of gloves.

'Right, get these on. There's an industrial estate just around the corner and stationed within are ten articulated trucks, each vehicle containing a cargo of top-notch designer gear. And none of your high street department store tack; it's mostly couture, mega expensive shit. Half a mill's worth in each truck, Armani, Gucci, Pucci, Marc Jacobs, Prada, Balenciaga, Chanel.'

'Couture?' I repeated, like it was a fabulously mysterious word I was hearing for the first time.

'Inside job. I've got the keys to one of the trucks. All we've got to do is drive the fucker over to one of the Sausage Man's lock-ups, unload the shit, and take a ten grand cut, cash up front. On Thursday we fly to Mexico City as planned, this is fucking it.'

I tried to take everything in, trucks, designer clobber, half a million, ten grand, Mexico? Fuck my head hurt from an overload of incendiary information, and on top of that I was bricking it.

'So no bank job?'

'Fuck that, too risky, bound to get caught, a mug's game. After this the world is ours, for a year or so anyway.'

That wasn't what he said the other day. Fuck me, what a fucked up state of affairs, but what could I do? I was caught up in the moment, fatal attraction to high risk criminality, and too late to back out. Anyway lifting a truckload of designer clothes was far less complicated than robbing a mother fucking bank. Shit, those impenetrable financial institutions were the bedrock of capitalism; its raison d'être, its secret formula, i.e. the uncanny ability to make money from thin air, and once caught bank robbers did more time than anyone, corrupt politicians, serial killers, mass murderers, even paedophiles.

The trucks stood dark and ominous in the faint glow of lamplight on an otherwise deserted industrial estate. Ronnie eyeballed the truck nearest and nodded.

'This is the one.'

He jumped up, opened the door, and signalled I follow suit. Once in the cab he checked the sleeping compartment.

'Just in case some muggy bonehead driver was in there,' he whispered afterwards.

'Blinding,' I whispered.

By the time we reached Baloney's lock-up we were nervous wrecks. Ronnie produced a key and opened the lock-up and we formed a chain to the truck and back. Expensive items of haute-couture flew through our arms in lightening fashion. Thirty minutes later it was job done.

'Right, now to get rid of the mother-fucking truck,' hissed Ronnie, 'Baloney will be waiting.'

Once again Ronnie drove and once again the truck was all over the place.

'Take it easy,' I cried out, after my head hit the windscreen.

'Nearly there, nearly there.'

We parked the empty truck outside some disused warehouses and legged it down a back street, where an edgy Baloney was waiting in a parked BMW.

'All sweet, yeah, sweet, sweet.'

'Yeah, yeah,' replied Ronnie.

All three of us were pumped up, heartbeats racing, the adrenaline flowing at supersonic rates. This was how it felt to be alive, to live in the moment, to learn how to fly. It was an amazing feeling, euphoric ecstasy, better than any drug high, even better than sex.

'Job done,' said Baloney once we were safely inside his drum.

Ronnie handed over the keys to the lock-up and Baloney pulled out a crumpled envelope from a drawer.

'Right, I don't want to be seen associating with either of you pricks until all the gear's been shifted, got it?'

We nodded.

'I'll let you know when the time is right, until then zero contact.'

'No worries Tone,' said Ronnie.

Baloney handed the envelope over and coughed. 'Here's your cut, five bags.'

'The deal was ten.'

'Deal's changed. Five now, five when I've shifted the merchandise.'

Ronnie tensed up and his hands formed into fists. I shot him a nervous glance and tensed myself. Ronnie ready-eyed Baloney.

'Are you taking the fucking piss?'

'It's the best I can do in the circumstances, take or leave.'

Ronnie closed his eyes and pressed a hand to his forehead. The atmosphere became fearsome, the tension unbearable. I began to shake, my breathing was unregulated, and a cold sweat coated my back. What the fuck was Ronnie gonna do? Finally Ronnie took his hand away and opened his eyes.

'Okay, forget the other monies, we don't want it.'

What did he mean, we?

Tony Baloney smiled nervously. 'What?' he replied, like Ronnie's words were completely incomprehensible, like he couldn't believe the reaction or non-reaction. Strangely, I knew exactly where he was coming from.

Ronnie's face remained a blank canvas, an iceman.

'If I can't have it now I don't want it.'

'You're nuts.'

'See ya later Tone.'

Outside Baloney's apartments Ronnie turned to me and said simply:

'Tomorrow we fly to Mexico.'

I gazed out of the aeroplane's cabin window. Far below, spread out in each direction, the lights of Mexico City blazed away, revealing another of the world's great metropolises. This was Mexico and we were free.

It was around midnight when we hailed a taxi from the airport and gave directions to a cheap downtown hotel. I gazed at the passing city scenes with wide eyes. The outer lying suburbs went on forever, dirty shacks, open sewers, shanty towns, stunning poverty clashing violently with stupendous wealth. Then we were driving through the historical centre, remnants of grander times, colonial architecture, the whiff off a forgotten past, packs of stray dogs roaming litter strewn side streets and dark alleys, food stalls, tacos, nachos, enchiladas, burritos, cheap and easy Mexican cuisine, the smells and aromas enticing and otherworldly, even the distant sound of old-fashioned mambo until finally, the fading glamour of the Hotel Dona Marina looming up into a hot night.

We checked into the hotel, an atmospheric building, cantina, courtyard, crumbling balconies, high ceilings. A sullen Mexican senora showed us to our room. She said nothing, but sighed as she climbed the marbled stairs like the world's burdens were all hers.

The room was street facing, had a balcony, and ancient furniture straight out of the 1930's. It looked like the Beats themselves had stayed there. Jack Kerouac, William Burroughs, Allen Ginsberg, Gregory Corso et al.

Decades pass in the blinking of an eye, I thought, and despite the relentless charge of modernity, some things never change. How many others had come before us, eager to see new things, new places, new horizons, at the beginning of another youthful Mexican adventure?

Ronnie gazed around, at the peeling wallpaper, the damp stains. 'Shit this room is beat, hasn't been renovated in decades. For all intents and purposes we have just walked into a timewarp. From now our past is forgotten. Fuck it, we don't even have a past.'

I threw myself onto a big brass bed.

'This bed is beat.'

Ronnie collapsed onto another bed.

'A motherfucking beat motel,' he mumbled semi-deliriously, 'and after this we just go, go, go, go...'

-19-

I awoke to different smells, exotic and unfamiliar. Ronnie was standing by an open window smoking a cigarette, looking like some character from a never-made Fellini movie. Outside, city sounds reverberated, car horns honked, disembodied shouts, calls and Spanish shrieks, Mexican grumblings, even a dog barking. It was the city, the Americas, it was life. I jumped out of bed, dashed to the window, and took a deep breath of that Mexican air. Then I zoned in on the streets.

'Man, look at this,' cried Ronnie excitedly. 'Come on we've got some exploring to do.'

We left the hotel and pounded the streets, wide-eyed, our hearts filled with expectation of the great unknown. Ronnie was talking.

'Over twenty million people reside in this fucker, the largest city in the Americas, and third largest on the planet. They call it Mexico City, but really it's Tenochtitlan, home of the Aztecs.'

An ancient flower lady prowled the sidewalk. Ronnie spotted her. 'Let's go get ourselves a flower and put it in our hair.' And with that hippy proclamation Ronnie was gone, running up the street and approaching the flower lady, who wasn't really a lady, but a soulful middle-aged senora with something eternal about her, something forever written into the worry lines on her bronzed forehead.

I watched as Ronnie proceeded to buy not one or two flowers, but great big armfuls of them, until only a handful of sorry looking specimens were left in the flower lady's great woven basket. A basket that could have been made in old Tenochtitlan, back in the days of Montezuma and the doomed

Aztecs, and for all I know it had been handed down from generation to generation, from one lonesome flower girl to another.

The flower lady thanked Ronnie over and over because now she no longer had to trudge the streets trying to sell a flower here and there, but could go home and talk to a friend on the telephone or just go for a walk in the park, or shopping, or whatever it is that flower ladies do when they no longer have any merchandise to sell.

Ronnie shoved an armful of bouquets at me and stuck two huge yellow flowers behind each ear. Then we set off down the road handing flowers to all and sundry, getting smiles from all the ladies, but also odd looks and stares. One surly man was so angered by our silly spontaneous act of generosity that he dashed his flower into the gutter, but we continued on our way regardless. The blistering streets of Mexico City teemed with people, characters milling around, tourists, locals, animals and whoever. Ronnie was animated, describing everything in melodramatic detail.

'Take it all in, look at that fat lady over there, waddling away, and those young lovers oblivious to everyone and everything just as they should be. And that old man and those pigeons, just the same as back home, and what about those moody Aztec warriors prancing around for tourists, but really going home and watching American TV, drinking Coca-Cola and wearing Nike shoes and Budweiser tee-shirts. And over there, check that, the alleged place where Cortes met Montezuma.'

'Really?'

'Of course and where the treacherous Dona Marina or La Malinche, even La Chingada lied and fucked her way into history and Freda Kahlo painted, and Diego Rivera drunk and

86

whored and DH Lawrence coughed, and old stumblebum Jack Kerouac and Burroughs searching for Yage an...'

'Dona Marina, that's the name of our hotel.'

Ronnie looked at me sideways, 'Yeah named after her, the great Mexican traitor, even with all that beauty.'

'And now we're here.'

'That's right that's right, following in ye old footsteps, let's go!'

We passed street sellers, their paltry wares spread upon old Inca rugs on the dusty sidewalks. Ronnie called a halt to proceedings.

'Now slow down a minute, this hombre is selling rocket knifes.'

I picked one up, pressed the button, a glinting blade shooting out. The market seller said something in guttural Spanish. Ronnie bargained with hand signals and other nonsense until the man just counted notes from his hand and wrapped the knives in old newspaper. Then he held up a pack of cards. It was a retro girly set. The grainy models looked like something straight out of the nineteen seventies. I brought two packs.

Restaurants and bars lined the cobbled streets and the pavements were littered with an assortment of street vendors and food stalls, the pungent aromas hanging in the air like an epicure's dream.

'Let's grab a taco or burrito from one of these beat stalls,' said Ronnie.

We approached a stall run by a fat sweating man who possessed an impressive enchilada and taco-enriched gut.

'Must love his munch,' said Ronnie, 'and so will know how to cook. Never trust a skinny chef, more interested in presentation than ingredients.'

I sidled up and listened in as Ronnie attempted to order two burritos with all the trimmings.

'El Grande, grande, everything on.'

The man got to work. Then I saw them, beers floating in a bucket of ice, golden and inviting. Unable to resist I reached in, pulled out two bottles, and handed one to Ronnie. The fat man smiled a true Mexico City smile and continued constructing the biggest burritos two western kids had ever seen or could have imagined. Ten minutes later the vendor handed over two gigantic burritos, crammed to bursting with steaming greasy mounds of grilled meat and vegetables.

'What the fuck are these monsters?' I said.

Ronnie attempted to put one end of the leviathan into his mouth.

'Burrito deluxe.'

After devouring our gargantuan burritos we pounded the hot, sticky, grime-stained Central American Latino streets. Ronnie put his arm around my shoulder.

'La Merced is our first destination, where the food market is, but more importantly the red-light district.'

At La Merced the scene was unbelievable. The market was huge and populated with a multitude of stalls selling every type of produce imaginable, mounds of produce, a myriad of different chillies, fresh fruit, vegetables, meat of every description, a cornucopia of food stuffs. We dashed along the aisles, wild-eyed and checking everything out. Ronnie could hardly contain himself.

'And look at this fruit, what the fuck is it? I've never seen anything like it. And here, a thousand different chillies. A mad multitude of chillies, each one hotter and fierier than the one next to it.'

'But where are the girls?'

'Fuck the girls, they can wait, what are they selling here?'

In front of us was a stall selling all things related to death, skeletons, masks, potions and herbs.

'Shit, this place is selling magic spells to ward off evil spirits and vanquish bad vibes. If only I could speak Spanish,'

We conversed with the owner of the stall, a pleasant middle-aged woman, and although she tried to help as best she could the language barrier defeated us.

'Maybe they can fuck that hex off that has been following us around.' said Ronnie, in between fruitless negotiations.

'I thought we left all that shit behind in London?'

'Maybe, maybe not, always best to err on the side of caution.'

Ronnie pointed to some mystery gear and accosted the stall holder. 'Magic spells, to cleanse and get rid of bad vibes.'

The woman laughed. 'Si, Si, Si.'

And neither of us were any the wiser.

We turned out of the market and along a sheltered side road. And there they were, the street walkers, hookers lining the sidewalks both sides of the road, an assortment of woman folk all available for a price, the eternal prostitute, the healer of man's ills, the great comforter.

We walked along slowly, eyeballing the girls on the sly and wondering. All shapes and sizes, ages, some mean, some cruel, some doomed, some you could even fall in love with, even the odd heavily pregnant woman.

'Shit,' said Ronnie, 'most of these women are fucked.'

'The prettier ones probably come out at night.'

'Look at that one, she must be at least fifty.'

We passed one battered, faded, and demented face after another, some strangely alluring despite the ravages of the precarious lifestyle and brutality of the oldest profession the world has ever known. We walked up and down that street two or three times wondering when to make our move, wondering what girls to choose and wondering what the hell we were doing there anyway.

'Shit, these whores are beat,' said Ronnie, after a woman with a huge pot belly grabbed him by the arm, and tried to drag him bodily up the narrow staircase of an equally beat La Merced hotel.

Ronnie was right; they were beat, even more beat than the junkie hookers of the ragged streets of East London, something I thought I'd never say.

'It must be the job,' I said.

'Of course it's not the job, it's the lifestyles. Anyway put up a line of shop workers or waitresses, even city high-flyers and it will be exactly the same. The young ones might possess a little bit of life, but the others will look completely insane. Ravaged by the day to day living, which destroys us all anyway.'

We continued getting come ons and incomprehensible offers in wild and wicked Spanish, Mexican, maybe even a little Aztec Nacthual, until we saw what we were looking for - a cantina, a drab affair named simply La Casa.

'Let's get a beer and discuss the matter in hand,' said Ronnie.

We stepped inside. The first thing I noticed were the cardboard skeletons hanging from the ceiling as if it were Halloween.

'What is this obsession with death anyway?'

'Death comes to us all,' replied Ronnie.

A hard-faced woman served us a couple of Sols. The bar was empty when we walked in, but within seconds a harem of scantily clad girls materialised from the shadows.

'Shit,' said Ronnie, 'we've walked into a brothel.'

There was no denying it. It had to be a brothel, but then the whole area appeared to be one long extended house of ill repute. The girls approached, eyeballing us all the way. They whispered to each other, laughed and giggled, smiled and pouted their red-smeared and lascivious lips. I ordered a couple of shots of tequila. Four girls surrounded me. Instead of two shots, six appeared.

'What the fuck?'

Ronnie handed the shots out to the girls.

'Don't worry, we buy drinks, they dance, and then we fuck. And look back here, some are little sorts.'

I downed my shot and took a swig of beer. Music played loud thumping electronic beats. Some of the girls danced.

'But what are the prices?

Ronnie had one girl hanging from his neck.

'Who cares, but get them to change the fucking musak, ask for a little mambo jambo.'

The sullen looks of earlier disappeared from the barmaid's face and she was now beaming. I ordered more bottles of Sol and tried to change the music.

'Mambo jambo, got any Perez Prado?' I yelled above the deafening din.

The girl understood nothing, but served more beer and produced a bottle of tequila and began pouring shots like it was the last night on God's mad earth. I didn't protest and decided to go with the flow. A full-figured bronzed sex-bomb grabbed me by the arm and spun me around. I heard laughter and clapping. The woman danced close and whispered in my ear.

'Come, amore, amore, we fuck NOW!'

I laughed and pulled away from those heaving brown breasts, one of which was elaborately decorated in a sinister tattoo. I grabbed a shot of tequila from the bar and handed it to the woman. She smiled a gold-toothed smile and tossed it off in one go. I was impressed and handed over another, which she tossed off again, but this time over her shoulder. It was crazy, insane, but where was Ronnie?

I found him in the arms of a beautiful whore whose eyes were like the dead of night, like the soul of old Mexico itself.

'I'm off to a boudoir amigo.'

What was this beauty doing working in a downtown beat brothel? She should've been draped elegantly across some expensive chaise lounge in the mansion of a millionaire husband, nails painted by a pretty Japanese maid, at her feet a Pekinese poodle. Then I saw the track marks on her arms and they told another story – if you were born into poverty then the fate of most poor girls, even the beautiful ones, was to live a life of wasted devastation. Born to lose.

'Okay, just be careful and look after your wallet.'

At that Ronnie pulled a face, as if remembering something important.

'Come with me to the toilet.'

In the stinking mosquito infested hombres Ronnie explained things.

'This is the plan. We take one brass at a time, just in case anything fishy is going on. The one who stays in the bar keeps hold of all the passports and money. Don't think anyone will do anything while we're at the bar, but once in the boudoirs it would be very easy for one of these lovely ladies to help themselves to an extra tip.'

'Good idea and maybe we should take it easy on the tequila?'

'Defo, stick mostly to beer and give the girls the shots. '

Ronnie handed his money bag over.

'Right, I'm taking that little Mexican princess upstairs, I might be gone some time. Hold the fort until my return.'

'Cheers amigo.'

I returned to the bar and the whores and contemplated matters. What had we done, escaped the mean streets of London to end up lying in the arms of Mexican prostitutes? Was that really the way we wanted to live? I wasn't sure and nothing seemed to matter. Our journey was just beginning. I ordered more tequila, handed out more shots, and again tried to change the music. It took a while, but after repeating the words Mambo Jambo and the name of the King of Mambo himself, Perez Prado, eventually I got a reaction.

The barmaid signalled to a young boy standing by the entrance, spoke a melodious stream of rapid Spanish, and the boy ran along the Aztec cobbled street at high speed. By now our antics had caught the attention of anyone who passed by La Casa and a crowd gathered in the doorway, men and women, and several curious street urchins.

Where was Ronnie? He'd been gone for an eternity and I was getting drunker and drunker. Let the good times roll. I pulled one of the skeletons from the ceiling and danced with it, while the girls formed a circle around me and cheered and yelled, obscene comments echoing off the walls and into the streets, and then I saw her. Where she came from I wasn't sure, but she was the one, young, early twenties, standing defiantly at the bottom of the staircase that led to a series of bedrooms. Her long glossy black hair tied back with a lovely white flower.

I wondered if it was one of those Ronnie had handed out earlier, a crazy thought, but who knows? The girl wasn't smiling or even touting for business. A sullen hostess. She stood at the bottom of the staircase glaring at me like she wanted to kill me.

Undeterred I marched over with a tequila bottle and handed her a shot. She took the glass and didn't drink the contents. Again, I wondered where Ronnie was and for one dreaded moment of paranoia I envisaged him lying naked across a dirty bed, his throat slit from ear to ear!

The mystery girl hung around. I tried to communicate, to ask her name, to get some form of recognition, but there was nothing, not even a smile. Maybe this beautiful and damned whore was a mute? I nodded towards the stairs and she reached out a slender brown hand, until our fingers touched and our hands clasped and I was living in a world filled with booze and skeletons and mysterious whores of an unforgiving night. I was alive.

I met Ronnie halfway up the stairs, drenched in sweat, his eyes bulging like those of a madman, a fiend.

'Now where d'ya think you're going amigo?'

Was this really my friend? He appeared like a demon, an imp, a crazy goblin of the night.

'Same place you've just been, the boudoir. Now here, take the valuables.'

Ronnie brushed the passports and wallets away with the wave of a boozy arm.

'Na, don't worry, this place is safe.'

'How d'ya know?'

'Coz I just had an epiphany in there.'

'An epiphany?'

'Yeah, I saw the fucking light. Nothing bad will happen to us ever again.'

Shit, Ronnie was losing it. All the signs were there, his increasing recklessness more than a little worrying.

'You sure you didn't just see the fucking pussy?'

'Well, I saw that also kid and that in itself was a small miracle.'

Ronnie saw the girl, crouching furtively behind me and let out a whoop of delight.

'Another epiphany amigo.'

He grabbed the girl's reluctant hand and smothered it in kisses, then ran off down the stairs screaming.

'More tequila, more girls, more mambo jambo!'

The girl and I tumbled into an empty boudoir. She sat on the bed and recommenced her glaring act. I walked to an open window and gazed at city night scenes. Down below, hookers of all descriptions prowled the balmy evening streets of La Merced. Night had fallen, a heavy scented darkness smelling of rotting food, death and pestilence. It was then that I understood the Mexican obsession with death, for everyone has to die, and we all die alone.

'Di nero,' said the girl.

I pulled out a wad of pesos. The girl took a few notes and stuffed them inside her exposed bra.

I undressed and lay down on the bed. The whore brought over a porcelain bowl and carefully washed my privates, checking for crabs amongst my tangled pubes. The white bowl had a circle of yellow chickens running along the inside rim, and I was filled with the sadness of life, the little inanimate chicks so young and carefree, and the Mexican whore so young and doomed, and me probably on the start of some long and convoluted road to oblivion. It all made sense, somehow.

Once the girl had completed the meticulous and tragic bed bath she stepped out of her knickers and lay down on the bed. I looked at what was before me. The slim brown legs, pubic hair trimmed neatly, red suspenders and black stockings, even the white flower pinning her black hair behind one ear.

I unclasped her bra with one deft action and out popped two perfectly formed brown breasts. I put my hand over one and kissed the girl. She responded and spread her legs. I got on top. The girl mumbled some words I didn't understand. Music could be heard, disembodied shrieks and cries, even snatches of mysterious conversation. I looked down at the girl and slid all the way in. The girl moaned and arched her back and dug her long nails into my back.

Afterwards we lay on the bed in each other's arms. The girl rested her head on my shoulder and was silent. I stared through the window. In the night sky was a star, just one, flashing dimly, a very old star, maybe as old as the universe itself. From the adjoining room came the sound of animalistic grunts and groans. I wondered if it was Ronnie.

The girl asked for more money. We fucked for hours. The night faded away, the city faded away, the brothel faded away, even Ronnie and the rest of the world faded away. It was like we were in our own little bubble, a pleasure dome of sweet debauchery...

-21-

I opened my eyes to find Ronnie staring at me in that fiendish way of his - his crazy eyes probing my soul. I was lying in the brothel bed, alone. Ronnie was drunker and madder than before. I avoided eye contact.

'Come on man, what the fuck you doing here, where's the girl?'

I didn't know where the fuck I was, let alone the girl. Sober now, it was more than possible that I'd dreamt her. I scanned the room and saw the bedside table, the moneybags, the passports and other important documents. I grabbed my wallet and checked the contents, a large wad of pesos bulged inside.

'Fuck knows, but at least she didn't rip me off.'

'Well of course not, the hex is gone, an the place has gone mad downstairs. The local Mafiosi have turned up, more girls, more music, but no more mambo jambo.'

'No more mambo jambo?'

'Fuck the mambo, I've met a couple of local dealers who've promised to sort us out some bona fide Acapulco gold, and at a very interesting price.'

'An interesting price.'

Ronnie bundled me down the stairs.

'Fucking dirt cheap amigo, now let's go.'

Downstairs, in the brothel, all types of Mexico City humanity mingled together, pimps, ponces, gangsters, tricksters, ordinary businessmen and workers, and more girls than ever before. The scenes were drunk and chaotic, and despite another posse of girls descending on us like fallen angels we made it to the counter to settle the bill. It was the same barmaid from earlier and she made a big deal out of charging us. She had this funny little adding-machine with a paper roll attached. She pounded buttons and the receipt grew bigger and bigger, until it flopped over the bar and down to the liquor-stained floor like a drunken snake.

I grabbed the bill and studied it with bleary eyes. There were numerous cervezas, tequilas, and Coca-Colas. Eventually the girl stopped adding. The bill came to over eight hundred dollars, expensive for any brothel, let alone a beat La Merced establishment. Ronnie pulled out a wedge of crisp American bills and handed them over, adding a $100 tip for the barmaid, who on seeing it kissed and hugged us like we'd just handed over a ticket to paradise.

'Let's get out of here,' growled Ronnie.

We shambled out of La Casa and into the hot stinking night. Darkness was everywhere. Two young Mexican men were instantly upon us.

'Amigo, amigo,' they hissed across the squalid and glistening cobblestones.

Straight away I was on my guard. Be streetwise, were the words that repeated themselves over and over. One glance was all I needed. They looked like a couple of desperate thieves and muggers and when Ronnie recognised them I didn't change my mind.

'These are the guys who can get us the good stuff.'

I fingered the rocket knife in my pocket and hoped Ronnie knew what he was doing. We had put ourselves in a vulnerable position, two gringos on their first night in Mexico City, drunk, with several thousand dollars' worth of traveler's cheques and banknotes on their immediate persons. I prayed the hex that had been following us around had indeed been exorcised in the seedy boudoirs of La Casa.

Ronnie struck up a slurred and whispered conversation. The guy spoke little English. I heard the word, si, repeated several times, and marijuana and Acapulco. The Mexicans looked shifty and devious. We were led into a gloomy side street, the carcass of a dead dog lay rotting in a watery gutter.

I pulled Ronnie back.

'Are you sure about this, why don't we wait until we've sussed the scene, this is dodgy.'

Ronnie dismissed my concerns with a drunken wave.

'Shut up, these guys are sweet. I've been drinking with them for hours while you fell in love with a tart.'

Fell in love with a tart? This throwaway comment angered and insulted me, but I said nothing. One of the Mexicans disappeared into the night. It began to rain then, large drops of water falling here and there, increasing in volume and density. I was getting wet.

'It's raining.'

Ronnie staggered and looked at me out of crazy bloodshot eyes.

'Didn't you hear what he said? The guy be back in a momento and a little fucking rain never hurt anyone.'

This was another comment that angered me, but still I said nothing. The rain graduated into a downpour. Pretty soon we were drenched, some congealed blood floated out of the rotting carcass of the dead dog. Where the fuck was the guy with the gear?

Two older men appeared. The young Mexican smiled treacherously.

'La policía.'

Immediately the older men were upon us. They shouted in Spanish; angry words ricocheting off the dark walls and buildings. Some dogs barked. Within seconds we were both kneeling in the rain. I saw the black flash of a revolver.

'No te mueve, o te mato!'

'De nero, gringo, De nero!'

I couldn't fucking believe it, not again, once more I was going to die before my time. The man pointed the gun and fired a stream of incomprehensible Spanish at us. Ronnie became remarkably calm. He pointed at me and shook his head.

'Hombre, no de nero.'

He produced a thin wedge of dollars. The man grabbed the dollars, smiled evilly, and pointed the gun again. A siren sounded and headlights appeared at the far end of the road. The guy with the gun waved the weapon in our direction. Certain he was going to shoot I closed my eyes and prayed for redemption. Then the sound of footsteps pounding cobbles and the voice of Ronnie.

'Quick, get up out of the fucking gutter and let's get the fuck outta here!'

I didn't need telling twice and stepped to it.

We ran splashing and reeling out of La Merced forever, grateful as the sound of the siren faded to nothing, and also thankful that our lives hadn't been taken away from us. Ronnie laughed and howled at the moon like a lunatic.

'What the fuck ya laughing at we could've been fucking laid down,' I said, as I slipped along the mean sidewalks of those late night unknown Mexico City streets, towards the sanctuary of the hotel Dona Marina.

Ronnie punched a fist into the air.

'Get that, held up at gunpoint and all they got was fifty fucking dollars!'

'All they got? I just had a gun waved in my face and all because you fancied a joint.'

'And guess what?'

'What?'

'I still fancy a joint.'

There I was in the beat bed of the beat Hotel Dona Marina, recollecting disconnected events from the mad night, and how lucky we were not to have lost all our money at the hands of gun-toting banditos. Maybe the hex had left us after all. But life is like that, fate, destiny, the roads travelled all the same, one wrong move and you're gone. I remembered La Casa and the scowling whore with the flower in her hair. I visualised her breasts and tender thigh as Ronnie snored and twitched in his sleep. A snapshot of making love to the sexy girl in the grimy boudoir played over and over inside my head. It didn't take long and I ejaculated silently, but pleasurably.

I wiped off on the bed sheet and recommenced thinking about stuff. I thought of home and Stupid and Angel and Ava, even that old dog Tony Baloney and the psychopathic Eyes Down. I wondered if I'd ever see them again or if I wanted to see them again, or if I would now spend the rest of my pre-ordained life on the road?

Ronnie awoke with all the answers. 'What a fantastic day and night in old Mexico City, deluxe burritos, the wonderful women of La Casa. That was a night to remember my friend, a legendary night but today we must leave for our time here is over.'

For once, I agreed with one of Ronnie's dramatic statements or ideas.

'Yep, I want to see the country and the ocean and organ pipe cacti and everything.'

'That's right amigo. Our next stop, Vera Cruz, four times heroic city, one or two nights there and then we'll check out some of those ancient Mayan pyramids dotted all over this mysterious land. After that we'll hit some old hippy-trail and find a deserted beach nestled somewhere on that there Pacific Ocean. Once established we'll partake of some peyote and see what visions are brought to us, and hope it leads to learn something about our spiritual selves and then...'

'Vera Cruz, Peyote?'

'I'll explain everything over breakfast.'

'But it's two o'clock in the afternoon?'

'Exactly, breakfast time.'

In the cantina of the hotel Dona Marina a lone girl was serving. She took one look at us and smirked.

'What's she smirking at?' said Ronnie.

'Fuck knows, maybe the word's out that a couple of green gringos got mugged in La Merced last night.'

'Impossible.'

The girl wound her way to our table. She was wearing a cute white apron and ragged leather huaraches, footwear that looked likely to disintegrate at any moment. She tapped Ronnie on the shoulder.

'Joo wan order'

'Yeah,' replied Ronnie, 'but we think a hex is on us and we want shot of it.'

The girl knitted her brown forehead, forming several attractive wrinkles.

'Ah hex?'

'Like bad vibes, evil spirits, a mother fucking curse.'

'Oh, oh, si, si, comphrendie, joo mia sister. She do goo, joo eat then joo mia sister, che help mia gringo.'

'Serious, she get rid of hex, I mean evil spirit?' said Ronnie.

'Si, si, joo safe in Mee-hee-co den.'

'Hey, hey, now ya talking, but first we must eat. Dos burrito deluxe and dos cerveza por favor senorita.'

After a hearty afternoon breakfast we found ourselves following the waitress of the Dona Marina hotel down some dark side alley. We'd caught a public bus to the outskirts of Zona Metropolitana del Valle de México, the greater metropolitan area of Mexico City, a vast never-ending scene of downtown suburbs and shanty-towns.

On the bus Ronnie posed the question.

'So what's your name baby?'

'Mia llamo Teresita.'

'That's almost the same as Kerouac's Tristessa, so I shall call you Tristessa.'

The girl fluttered her eyelashes before punching Ronnie hard on the arm.

'No, Teresita gringo or I keel joo!'

Ronnie grabbed his arm and winced. 'Fiery,' he mumbled afterwards.

We came to a run-down block of crumbling apartmentos, living quarters for the poor and disenfranchised of Mexico City. This was where Tristessa's sister lived. We climbed the concrete stairs one by one. It reminded me of an East End council estate, only more colourful. Some doors were painted in pastel colours, a hint of brightness clashing ferociously against the general deprivation. Some ragged nut brown children entertained themselves in the squalid environs of a gloomy stairwell.

We were led into a sparsely furnished living room with zero natural light. Tristessa's sister was slumped across a busted sofa watching a battered television set, she was either stoned or insane. Tristessa spoke in Spanish at some length, encouraging her sister to jump up and switch the television off. Then she dragged two chairs into the centre of the room, all the while yapping away in Mexican.

'Joo sit here,' instructed Tristessa.

We sat.

Moments later we were stationed on a couple of busted up chairs while Tristessa's crazy crackhead sister sprinkled green herb-like stuff around us. She screamed and rambled while she sprinkled. Two scraggy cats appeared to observe the scene. Ronnie sniffed the air and shot me a sceptical glance.

'Can you smell that?'

'Smell what?'

'Basil.'

The unmistakable herbal aroma was all around. A huge bowl of spaghetti bolognaise loomed up before me.

'Who gives a shit?'

'You're right nothing matters.'

Ten minutes later it was all over. Tristessa's sister shrieked and rambled, went into a feigned trance-like state and ended her performance by executing a neat little rain dance or sun dance or hex dance. And then, according to Tristessa, we were completely and utterly hex-free.

'Si, si, si now joo safe in a mia mee-hee-co gringos.'

'Cuanto-es?' asked Ronnie.

'Diez Yankee dollar.'

Ronnie pulled out a twenty.

'And the hex is finito, kaput?'

Tristessa placed her hands on hips and pouted.

'Si, kaput!'

Bargain,' said Ronnie and handed over the twenty, which Tristessa hurriedly stuck down her bra before her sister was able to see the denomination.

'Adios Tristessa,' said Ronnie.

Tristessa ran up and punched Ronnie on the arm again, hard.

'Mia llamo Teresita!'

-23-

The bus drove through one tiny Mexican mountain village after another, strings of pretty-coloured electric bulbs illuminating the primordial darkness as the vastness of that fantastic megalopolis Mexico City became just another memory. People gathered outside porches of white-washed adobe shacks, some just sitting there blank-faced, others engaged in animated conversations with their friends and family and neighbours.

'So why are we going to Vera Cruz?' I said.

'Dunno, I just liked the sound of the name, Vera Cruz, the True Cross, Four Times Heroic City.'

'Four Times Heroic?'

'They repelled attacks on the city by the Spanish, the French, even the Yanks. And there is something to be said for fighting for what you believe in.'

From then on Ronnie and I hardly spoke, we just stared out of the windows into the gloaming, wrapped snugly in a couple of airline blankets. Ronnie looked like a little fellaheen of the midnight Mexican road, eyes glued to the window, occupied by unknown thoughts.

The people here were more Indian than the typical mestizo Mexican, indigenous folk, descendants of the Aztec and Maya living proof they still inhabited Mexico and always would. Some cats and dogs wandered around, and every now and then the pretty face of a shy Indian girl appeared fleetingly in the window of a passing shack or cottage. And finally, just before I closed my eyes, an old man wearing a sombrero, weathered face, leading a half-starved burro along a winding dirt track. A holy Mexican illumination.

On reaching Vera Cruz the night was dark and still, but

somewhere something was happening. As we hit the streets in search of another beat motel, the soft sounds of gentle music were carried to us on sea breezes infused with the briny smell of the ocean.

Ronnie and I trekked the lonely sea-front road, backpacks over our shoulders, eyes peeled.

'Can you smell that?' said Ronnie.

'Smell what?'

'The smell of victory my friend.'

It was past midnight by now and it took a long time searching around for suitable and affordable accommodation. Finally, after an hour or so, we found a small waterfront hotel and decided to call it a night. The hotel was a bland non-descript affair, but the room was large and breezy, and through the only window the waters of the port were reflected in romantic harbour lights.

We chucked our backpacks to the floor and hit the beds. We lay there talking into the small hours until we didn't have the energy to muster up any further conversation. Then we just lay there saying nothing and thinking our own little mundane thoughts of eternity.

The following morning we set out at once to explore the town.

Vera Cruz was a strange mixture of old and new, neither beautiful nor ugly, and we wandered the hot streets in an aimless, but contented fashion. At lunch we brought a couple of cold beers and tacos and gazed at the turquoise waters of the Caribbean Sea. The old Spanish fort of San Juan de Ulúa sat just across from us, divided by a long boardwalk. We strolled over and found a couple of ancient cannon pointing towards the sea. We sat astride a canon each and munched our tasty tacos and swigged our rapidly warming booze.

'I've had an idea,' said Ronnie casually as he gazed across the parapet of the castle and into the blue yonder.

'Yeah?'

'Travelling by bus is all well and good, but I think the next leg of our journey should be by car.'

'A taxi will be far more expensive than a bus.'

'I mean buy a car, drive ourselves, you know get to see the country and the people close at hand.'

'But I can't drive.'

'I've already considered that and reckon I'm more than capable of doing all the driving.'

'Serious?'

'Serious, and anyway we'll just use it to drive from one side of the country to the other. Once we've hit the Pacific we'll sell it and plot up in some lonesome and romantic beach hideaway. What d'ya think?'

'If you think you can do it, I mean what about all the Spanish road signs and asking directions and shit?'

'Piece of piss. Come on, let's check out the downtown Zocalo where all the night life is to be experienced. Afterwards we'll see about getting ourselves a motor.'

As we headed downtown the sky transformed. An armada of menacing grey clouds converged on the near horizon and headed inland to do battle with the city.

'Don't like the look of those clouds,' I remarked.

By the time we reached the downtown plaza, lined with arcades, houses, cafes and bars, the entire sky had lowered several hundred feet and day turned to night. Huge raindrops descended from the heavens, one of which was enough to soak a man, and the wind picked up dramatically.

'Quick let's slip inside one of these cantinas, looks like we're in for a storm,' said Ronnie.

Once inside the sanctuary of the cantina we plotted up at a window seat and watched events as they unfolded. Townsfolk and market sellers emerged to protect their wares from the adverse weather conditions, and within seconds a full-blown tropical storm hit. The rain literally danced upon the sidewalks. Fierce winds rattled the glass in the windowsills and bent palm trees ninety degrees. A barman observed the storm.

'Hurricanas,' he said simply.

Two hours and two nursed beers later it was all over. It had been exciting to watch, but as the skies cleared and the rains dissipated, the havoc wreaked upon the port was revealed. Awnings blown away from buildings, palm fronds strewn across roads, even a small boat lifted over the sea wall and deposited unceremoniously in the middle of the street. And aside from this devastation the roads and side streets were immersed in several feet of murky water.

'Shit, how we gonna get back to the hotel?' I said.

Ronnie slipped off his plimsolls and rolled up his jeans.

'Looks like we gonna have to swim.'

We left the cantina and waded along a water-logged highway. In places, the water reached above our knees. And it wasn't just that, it was something else, the water a sickly brown, unidentifiable objects floating amongst the opaque river.

I pulled my tee-shirt over my nose to deflect the overpowering stench. 'This is getting ridiculous,' I said.

'See any river taxis?'

'Nope.'

As we stood there, waist deep in what can only be described as raw sewage, a persistent psst psst caught my attention.

'Amigo,' said a voice.

Leaning against a wall, a one-legged Mexican.

I nudged Ronnie.

'That guy over there, with the one leg, he's calling us.'

'Ignore the fucker.'

We began wading away, but the man called out once more.

'Amigo's, joo stay Hotel Sans Cristobel, no?'

'Yeah, so what?'said Ronnie.

'Amigo's I joo friend, come, joo follow me, I know dry road.'

'How much?'

The one-legged man shrugged his shoulders and adopted a philosophical expression.

'I joo friend remember, ba spare few pesos, no?'

'Thought so,' said Ronnie. Then he glanced at his immersed legs. 'Fuck it, it won't be much and I don't fancy getting trench foot.'

'Good idea,' I said, as we waded over to the cripple.

The man re-balanced with the use of a wooden crutch and held out a dirt-grimed hand.

'Joo name amigo?'

I shook his hand.

'Joseph'

'Ronnie,' said Ronnie, 'and yours?'

'Mia Hugo, Hugo Santamaria.'

-24-

We followed the one-legged Mexican along a maze of inundated back streets and winding alleys.

'Where you from amigos?'

'The Cockney Republic,' said Ronnie.

A quizzical expression adorned Hugo's boat.

'De Cockley Republica, this I never ere, how long you stay Vera Cruz?'

'One, maybe two days.'

'Of course this no long.'

'We think it is.'

'An then where amigos?'

'Further.'

'Further? I like.'

At some point our impromptu guide turned into a grimy underground precinct lined with gloomy shops and shadowy stalls. He stopped outside a grubby-looking cantina.

'Amigos, joo wan eat?'

'In there?'

'Si, is good food, local, real Mexican food.'

'Fuck it,' said Ronnie, 'let's take a risk.'

As soon as we crossed the threshold three or four Mexican waitresses surrounded us. They all knew Hugo.

'He brings a different tourist here each day,' said Ronnie.

'Probably working on commission.'

'Defo.'

'Still, he's a likeable chap.'

'A diamond geezer.'

There was no menu, but when Hugo spoke to the waitress in Spanish and translated Ronnie called a halt to proceedings.

'Hugo, order for the three of us and makes sure to order plenty of different dishes.' Then he smiled at the waitress and waved an arm in the general vicinity of the table: 'Senorita, tres cerveza por favor.'

The waitress clapped her hands and a short time later dishes of steamy aromatic Mexican cuisine arrived at our table, along with cold beers. Hugo was right, the food was good and tasty, unlike anything we had so far eaten, and we wasted no time in making gluttons of ourselves.

'This is the best food we've eaten in Mexico Hugo, make sure to give my compliments to the chef,' said Ronnie.

Hugo smiled broadly and gave his rotund stomach an affectionate pat.

'Ah Mama Rosita's de best food Vera Cruz, an Hugo Santamaria know what he like.'

'And Senor Ronnie Perrot knows what he likes.'

As we devoured the tasty meal Ronnie broached the subject of buying a car to Hugo.

'You like buy car amigo?'

'Yeah,' replied Ronnie, 'a cheap second-hand one, both reliable and durable. I want to drive to the other side of Mexico, you know the Pacific side.'

Hugo's eyes lit-up.

'I can car, good car mia brother an good price, this car take anywhere joo wan, even Honduras.'

'And what exactly is a good price, Hugo?'

Hugo glanced from side to side, rubbed his huge gut, and spoke frankly.

'I thing Senor Ronnie, five hundred dollars good price no?'

'And when can we see the car?'

'Si, meet manana hotel.'

'Excellent,' said Ronnie. Then he signalled to one of the

waitresses, 'senorita, trez cerveza por favor.'

'Where go nochas?' asked Hugo.

'Not sure, thought we'd hit the downtown Zocalo and observe the scene.'

'If joo wan we tour Nochos Vera Cruz, an joo wan women, a la concha.'

'Where can we meet?' said Ronnie.

'Si joo hotel, tonight?'

'It's a date.'

That evening, whilst waiting for Hugo Santamaria to show up at the hotel, I gazed out over the Caribbean Sea. Ronnie was playing solitaire and for once in an uncommunicative mood. I leaned out of the window and thought about stuff, like where the time goes or what does the future hold or what might become of me or Ronnie in the long run, the big life questions, endlessly fascinating, endlessly unanswered, the limits of man's reason providing nothing but tantalising mysteries. A tanker, silhouetted by a big yellow moon, made its way slowly out of the port of Vera Cruz and across the Gulf of Mexico - deck lights twinkling into the night like sirens. I wondered where it was bound and marvelled at the machinations of human activity, all the commerce, the coming and going, the ceaseless industrial production. What part did I play in all that, a young man from East London, one of the great metropolises of the world? Where was my walk on part in the great stage of life? Was it possible for an individual to indeed drop out, walk the earth, with no interest in the pursuit of money or material possessions? The capitalists, it appeared, wanted everyone to work to buy things they didn't need or worse couldn't afford so as to be indebted to them for life and subsequently enslaved for life. But who were they and what did they want with me? Total self-sufficiency seemed the only possible answer, but others before me had followed that path and failed, but maybe it was the answer, maybe...

It was late evening and the sky was a deep crimson and purple when I saw him, our new friend, hobbling along the cobbled sidewalk. I called down.

'Hugo.'

A gold tooth flashed into the night.

'Amigo, joo ready big night Veracruz?'

'Hell, yes.'

Out on the streets it was an electric night, the atmosphere infused with energy and the sensuality of the tropics, the prospect of romance.

'We go Zocalo, Jarochos, Veracruz, drink, eat, an jus watch ee worl go by,' Hugo told us.

Nightfall had transformed the Zocalo into a bustling crucible of exotic happenings. Families strolled along, street traders plied their wares, and bands of Mariachis strummed silver-stringed guitars.

We found a bar close to the edge of the Zocalo and watched couples dancing across a black and white marbled floor illuminated by electric light. The couples danced to the rhythms of the Caribbean, salsa, marimba, and reggae. We ordered bottles of Dos Equis beer and small cigars and sat there watching the action, drinking and smoking happily.

And then a different music played, strange and graceful whereupon a ritualistic dance commenced, like none that had gone before. Hugo leaned over and spoke in whispers.

'That amigos is Danzon, especial dance of Vera Cruz. Ee come from Cooba many time ago, but now ours an ours alone. See how de couples react to each other, is beautiful an passionate no?'

We watched transfixed. I thought of all those dark and dingy discos in London, pounding out Dalek musak while the catatonic clientele consumed as many drugs as possible so as to be able to feel something. Ronnie leaned over.

'This is what it's all about, there are different scenes and attitudes to be witnessed and experienced. London's fucked, over-populated and filled with the world's detritus. It doesn't seem English anymore, just the perfect nightmare vision of a big city.'

Ronnie was right and I was glad we had left, but the longer we were away the less a return to that life, to that way of living seemed possible or even feasible. I wanted more out of life, a more satisfying experience, before I grew old and faded away. I wanted to feel something. Hugo, gazing at the dancers, became misty-eyed.

'An before mia motorcycle accident, mia great dancer, el best.'

'I'm sorry about your accident Hugo,' I muttered feebly.

Hugo puffed on his cigarillo and took a swig of beer. 'Don sorry Josep, what done is done. In that time el fates conspire against Hugo Santamaria, ba Hugo Santamaria live an fight another day.' He pointed to a collection of large ships and boats moored some distance in the harbour, 'Is good joo ere amigos, tonight big night Vera Cruz.'

'Why's that?'

'See la ships, Americano merchant navy an Korean navy. Sailors a sea, two, three month an more - an spend, spend amigo, the ladies of La Linea happy tonight. Come we eat.'

'What's on the menu?'

'Mia local delicacy amigos, huachinango a la Veracruzaña.'

'Huh?'

Hugo clapped his hands and set off down the narrow road, 'Pescado, gringos, pescado!'

25

Huachinango a la Veracruzaña, a delicious dish of red snapper covered in a fiery tomato sauce, which we ate in a beat cantina hidden at the top of a cobbled alley just off the main square. Hugo discussed the second-hand car proposal while we crammed our mouths with olives, fish, capers, and tiny triangles of toasted bread.

'Car, joo still wan, Senor Ronnie.'

'Yep, we haven't changed our mind.'

'Okay, ba no can joo car.'

Ronnie looked up in surprise, 'But you said...'

'Mia brother, he sell already, ba nuevo idea joo like?'

'Give me the low down Hugo.'

Hugo dabbed at his mouth with a large serviette that was tucked into the open neck of his Hawaiian shirt.

'Bueno, it like dis. Mia friend go San Cristóbal de las Casas. Es highlands in Chiapas, an very close Mayan ruins of Bahlam Kin, loss city Jaguar Sun. He someone help drive. Say joo go wit him an mia go, for mia never go.'

'This sounds ideal, when is he leaving and what will the cost be?

'Manana. For joo is cheep, just help wit drive, an pay la gas.'

Ronnie raised his bottle.

'I'll drink to that, to the next stage of our trip and to our new friend Hugo who comes with us.'

After dinner we marched to the Zocalo and flitted from bar to bar, drinking beers and shots of cheap Tequila straight out of caballito glasses with neither salt or lime, which Hugo told us was a crazy gringo way to drink Tequila anyway. Then we were in the red-light district, passing groups of hookers plying their trade amongst the shadows of La Linea, the strip.

'Ah more brasses,' yelled Ronnie, 'women have been selling themselves since before the conquistadors, since before the Aztecs and Maya, and way back to an even more primitive people.'

Hugo smiled. 'Joo like girls amigos?'

'No, no, we just want to party, take us to a club, somewhere we can dance.'

I clapped my hands. 'Yeah, we wanna dance all night long!'

'Si, si, vamoose.'

At the next corner, standing outside a strip club, we stumbled across a queue of Korean sailors. They were dressed in traditional navy uniforms, like a bunch of Asian Frank Sinatras and Gene Kellys out on that there town.

'See amigos,' cried Hugo, 'Jack tar spen all money one long unforgettable night ere Vera Cruz.'

Hugo led us to a back entrance of the club, where he negotiated entry with a surly doorman, and then we were in without having to queue or even pay a cover charge. A door opened onto a cavernous club setting, deafening salsa music blasting out of hidden speakers, and crowds of Korean sailors and American merchant navy guys jostling and mingling. On a series of podiums naked girls gyrated and flaunted their bodies to rhythmic Latin beats.

'Jesus Christ,' I said. 'A gigantic lap-dancing club.'

'Twenty lovely ladies stripping all at once. It's like the land of the tits!'

The stage was lined with voluptuous Mexican girls, peeling off clothes, giving it all they had for hundreds of leering, ecstatic sailors, busy sticking wads of notes into suspenders and knickers. The night flew by in a drunken whirl of dancing, ogling naked women, and shots of tequila. We wandered the club, gazing at pert tits, bronzed thighs, and glistening cunts. We watched dance after dance, striptease after striptease, the girls leaving nothing to the imagination. The tequila flowed and the bright lights flashed.

The mounds of shaking flesh on show became too much for Hugo and Ronnie, and they went in search of a brothel. Outside the night was dark and iridescent. In our absence there had been another tropical downpour, puddles everywhere, surface water sparkling in the night like black diamonds. Hugo led us to his favourite casa, a grimy block of crumbling pastel-coloured apartments at the dark end of a litter-strewn downtown alley.

Inside the bordello, a fat man dressed in a beer-stained wife-beater sat behind a rickety desk, a circle of flies buzzing above his head oblivious to all the carnality going on, or maybe attracted to it. Elsewhere, an assortment of girls and clients wandered hallways and landings, disappearing into rooms or sashaying up and down a wooden staircase. Hugo spoke to the fat man and moments later a whore with jet-black hair and pouting lips smothered in layers of crimson lip-stick appeared in a doorway. The tart beckoned Hugo inside with a business-like jerk of the head. Seconds later Ronnie was taken away by an Indian girl dressed in a see-through yellow slip, no more than sixteen or seventeen. As I stood in the doorway of the brothel an ugly ancient whore with a bloated belly lunged at me with grasping paws, hissing lewd words in Spanish. I slipped free of her despairing grasp and got out of there.

Another drink that's what I needed, and forgetting all about Ronnie and Hugo I went in search of a bar. It was late by now. I wandered from street to street until the sound of music escaping from an opened door drew me towards it. I entered a small bar. In a far corner a young Mexican dude played western pop songs on a small keyboard, *Light My Fire*, by the Doors. He wasn't very good and nobody was listening. I felt sorry for him, bashing out his lonesome music in a bar at the end of the world. And then for all the other struggling musicians playing out the same melancholy scene in crumby bars and clubs from there to Timbuktu.

I ordered some bottles of beer to take away. Outside the bar of nothingness I became disorientated. Where was the brothel? And where was my hotel? Drunk I hardly cared and wandered the streets aimlessly, happily observing the early morning Vera Cruz scenes. A gang of whores passed by, touting for business, shrieking heartfelt and desperate pleas in Spanish, but I just smiled and walked on, while the curses rang out behind me like a manic and debauched libretto. I reached the port and saw the ocean reflected in the harbour lights. I sat on the harbour wall and supped my beer.

And then I saw them, Hugo and Ronnie ordering tacos or burritos or enchiladas from a roadside stall. Just the sight of my two friends and my heart rejoiced. I was no longer lost and alone in the world. I bounded over with joyous leaps.

'Ronnie!'

Ronnie turned around, along with a visibly drunk Hugo.

'Burrito deluxe?'

I took the burrito and handed him a beer.

'Cerveza?'

The three of us sat on the harbour wall, devouring our tasty burritos, and sharing the last bottles of beer.

'So where the fuck did you go?' said Ronnie.

'I got bored amigos, bored of waiting for you two freaks to finish, so went in search of another beer.'

Ronnie smiled and glanced to Hugo, who was putting more of the burrito down his front than in his mouth.

'Hugo, what time we leave tomorrow?'

'Manana,' burped Hugo between mouthfuls.

The sky was beginning to lighten, a band of grey and pink rising steadily. I pointed to the horizon.

'But Hugo, it's already manana, no?'

Hugo adjusted his battered crutch, gazed unsteadily at the sky, and burped again.

Ronnie smiled a gruesome smile.

'A belch is the answer to all life's mysteries. Now, for the first time in our lives, we understand the meaning of all things.'

26

We waited for Hugo all day in the hotel room. Had we missed our new friend? Was he driving to Chiapas to visit the ancient Mayan ruins of the city of the Jaguar Sun, paying respects to his long lost ancestors without us? Then I wondered why those ancient Mayan and Aztec civilisations collapsed and disappeared or why their inhabitants abandoned those great classical centres. Everything changes. Civilisations rise and fall, the ancient Egyptians, Greece, The Roman Empire, the Olmecs, the Aztecs, the Maya. Everything must pass. I thought about London and home. I wondered what Ava was doing or Angel or Baloney, even that murderous dog Eyes Down. Then I forgot about all that and looked to the future. Soon this holiday, this great Mexican adventure would be over. What would my next move be?

Sometime during the afternoon Ronnie did a beer run and returned with a few bottles of Dos Equis. We sat around and drank them slowly, easing our brutal hangovers, and chasing those melancholy blues away.

Ronnie had his nose deep in Oswald Spengler's *The Decline of the West*. He said that Spengler's idea that civilisations were of a cyclical nature explained the decline of the Aztec and Mayan empires. I'd brought a handful of books by my favourite poets, and while Ronnie wrestled with the complexities of Spengler's weighty tome I perused a slim volume of poetry by the Chinese master Li Po. Stars appeared in a black Caribbean sky and distant music was carried to us on gentle sea breezes. I gazed at the blue tropical stars and read a poem about a boy moon gazing, who in the morning would have to get up early for work in a paddy field. The poem affected me greatly and I knew I'd never forget it, for I was once that boy.

Later my thoughts returned to what I would do once the Mexican dream was over. Go to college? Get a job, find a girl and settle down? Or maybe I'd travel the world forever, going from one country to the next without ever settling down, a global hobo, a wanderer of the endless highway earth. I thought about Australia and my one year work visa. With Ronnie by my side things would surely work out. Further, always further, for once started we had to keep going, following the road wherever it led right to the very bitter end.

And then I remembered Angel and how pretty she was until the disembodied, but instantly recognisable voice called out loud and clear.

'Amigos, amigos...'

We rushed over to the window. Down below on the dusty sidewalk, leaning on his rickety crutch, a certain Hugo Santamaria. Next to him a black Volkswagen, engine running, unidentified driver at the wheel.

We grabbed our bags, checked out of the hotel, and clambered into the waiting vehicle. The car drove into the night, leaving the four times heroic city and its passionate inhabitants far behind forever.

Hours passed. The Mexican night was dark and sticky, and for the first hundred or so kilometres Hugo and Ronnie slept like babies. As for the driver, he never spoke a word, eyes glued to the white line in the middle of the road. You could understand the universe just by staring at those disappearing lines. Everything is devoured eventually. Life eats itself.

Like modern day Célines we continued our journey into the night. Gradually, despite the discomfort of the cramped quarters, my eyelids grew heavy. The road passed through impenetrable jungle on both sides, the silhouettes of agaves bushes and trees whirring by, dark, mysterious, and hallucinatory.

Something prodding me in the leg awakened me. I opened one tired eye and squinted. It was the driver, Hugo's non-communicative and mysterious friend. Outside was primordial darkness, the roadside desolate. The driver pointed to Ronnie, scrunched on the backseat, fast asleep. I glanced at Hugo. His one and only leg was propped up on the glove compartment, gentle snores escaping from his pursed lips. The man gesticulated with greater urgency. He looked incredibly tired, bloodshot eyes, pained features, the embers of another Mexico night glowing incandescent.

I gave Ronnie a sharp nudge and his body twitched involuntary. He opened his eyes in startled bemusement.

'What the f...'

'Your time to drive amigo.'

The driver made a driving motion, and placed both hands to the side of his head to indicate sleep. Seconds later Ronnie was firmly ensconced in the driver's seat, fidgety, nervous, perpetual motion.

'Man, could do with a livener,' he bawled above the roar of the battered Volks engine.

'A livener?' I bawled.

'Yeah, you know some good foot, bugle, even some speeeeed.'

With the engine roaring Hugo awakened from his comatose state, his eyes red, the circles underneath sad and dark, his black hair dank and lifeless.

'Amigos, amigos, wha has...'

He glanced over his shoulder and caught sight of his sleeping friend.

'Ah, si, si, drive senor Ronnie an mi guide.'

'How far to go?'

Hugo adjusted his leg.

'Mucho kilometre, but if drive fast an no stop, God willing Bahlam Kin before sun rise. Do hafe cerveza?'

Ronnie pulled the car back onto the highway.

'No.'

Hugo pulled something from his shirt pocket.

'Too bad, es good hafe plenty jale.'

'Jale?'

Hugo held up a small plastic bag, filled with white powder. Ronnie slapped his hands down hard on the steering wheel.

'Yee-ha, now you're talking Hugo. I was just saying to Josep back there, how I could do with some good foot.'

Hugo was confused. 'Goo foo?'

'Yeah, good foot Hugo, bugle, devil's dandruff, even your good old Jale.'

Hugo smiled another of his trademark gold and ruby toothed smiles, before coining a small mound up a nostril and heaping another mound of cocaine onto the coin and passing it to Ronnie.

Ronnie didn't even have to take his eye off the road. He sniffed and held his head back.

'Let's go!'

Hugo handed the jale to me.

'Ya, si,si Josep, jale, jale, buena onda, buena onda.'

I glanced at the contents of the bag. Outside it remained dark, but it would soon lighten and I didn't want to miss anything. I scooped a pile of the white stuff onto the peso and sniffed it up both nostrils. It hit almost instantaneously. Hugo winked.

'Now joo drive Ronnie, an no stop. Sunrise bess time see Maya an sacred home mia ancestors, vamoose!'

-27-

Now everything was stardust, the car, our faces, the road, the countryside, everything. We were moving, wide-awake, wired-up, and determined to get to Bahlam Kin without the need for another break. Ronnie drove that old Volks at top speed and the Mexican landscape flashed by, mountain ranges, volcanoes, and miles and miles of featureless jungle.

Hugo snorted coke at regular intervals and laughed and joked. He tuned the car radio into a station playing the latest Mexican pop music and kept up a rapid stream of broken Spanglish. After a while I was no longer able to understand a word of what he was saying and just nodded my head and yay-sayed at regular intervals. I pounded the window of the car, bongo style. Ronnie concentrated on the road, accelerator down, face set, beating out a miniature bongo beat on the steering wheel, fingers tapping madly, completely in time with me like telepathy.

Our vehicle approached a long line of cars, caught behind some unseen obstruction up ahead. Ronnie eyed the traffic.

'Fuck it, look at that shit, gonna hold us up.'

'Don't worry, we'll make it,' I yelled.

Ronnie put his foot down, revved the engine, and dropped several gears.

'Go old car go!'

He pulled the ancient Volks onto the other side of the highway and arrowed forwards. We overtook cars, one two, three four. Hugo sat up.

'Mia gringo whaaaaaaaaaaaaaaaaa.'

Ronnie whooped and pointed madly at the cars as we zoomed past, trailing stardust everywhere.

'Go, go, go mother-fucking go!'

The Volks was travelling now, nuts and bolts rattling, axle creaking, tyres burning rubber. I fell into some sort of trance state. The stardust, all I could see was stardust, sparkling like diamonds, like super-string scattering magnetic radiations. Life was everywhere; death was everywhere, diameter to wave length, spherical particles. We flew onwards, always onwards, over the cusp of the hill and continuing. Hugo pulled out his bag of jale and passed it around. All three of us took a big toot, all except Hugo's silent friend asleep beside me, looking more dead than alive, a cadaver.

'We Bahlem Kin fe sun rise gringo!'

'We'll get there, we'll get there.'

Then up ahead, a mile or so away, a Mack truck, dust clouds billowing, headed towards us, while on the other side of the road a long line of intermittent traffic.

'Look at that truck, better pull over,' I said.

'Fuck it, we'll make it.'

The truck got closer and there was no gap on the other side. Hugo stopped snorting coke and stared straight ahead. He issued frantic Spanish words, hands clasped together.

'Pull over, pull fucking over,' I screamed.

Ronnie shook his head. 'No fucking way, it's me against the fucking truck.'

This is it, I thought. I'd got to Mexico, but was going to get killed before I'd even seen any of it, and all because I was in a car driven by a madman. The truck loomed up. The stardust evaporated. Ronnie revved the engine and dropped a gear.

'There's a gap up ahead!'

There was a small gap, but we'd never make it, suicide to even try. I tried to speak, but no words emerged, I was petrified. Hugo pulled out a set of rosary beads and ran them through his fingers. The truck got closer and closer, a gruesome death nearer and nearer. Fuck it, I could make out the trucker's face, brown and bloated, grinning like a maniac, one arm waving frantically.

I was dead and it didn't matter. Ronnie dropped another gear, revved the engine, hands clasped tight on the steering wheel, white knuckles, aiming the car at the tiny shrinking gap. The truck sounded its horn, an extended toot, the blast of destiny. I closed my eyes. Ronnie whooped and yelled with delight. I opened my eyes. There was the truck, disappearing into the distance. We had made it.

'You cunt you nearly killed us.'

'Live a little. Did you see it, did you see that poetry? It was motherfucking beautiful! Someone loves us man, they really do.'

I didn't reply to this, but reflected on Ronnie's nascent pathological recklessness. Something would have to give some-day, that much I did know, but he was right that the overtake had been beautiful.

Several hours of non-stop driving later and the eastern horizon grew lighter, turning shades of grey and then salmon pink, followed by an explosive red and gold sunrise. Ghostly images loomed up on either side of the dusty road, shacks, cottages, phantom birds, iguanas perched on fence posts and rusty barbed wire like reptile sentries. The road passed through miles of extensive farmland, Mayan villages, and endless jungle. And then a strange town emerged out of nowhere, shrouded in wreaths of mist.

It was early morning, but already the townsfolk were up and about, conducting everyday business and routines. As we cruised the main street something caught Hugo's attention. He told Ronnie to stop the car.

'What, why?'

Hugo pointed to a small store.

'Bahlam Kin no far now, an we stop for refreshment si?'

'Shit yeah, some drinks, maybe even a burrito or two.'

'Come we go.'

I glanced at Hugo's friend. He remained asleep, the likelihood of his ever awakening after the crazy events he had slept through appearing remote.

'What about your friend, shall I wake him?'

'No, Hesus sleep, he drive more more, when we left you.'

'What do you mean, when we left?' asked Ronnie

Hugo hopped towards the store.

'Si, after Bahlam Kin, mi an Hesus we hafe go on alone.'

'Shit, Hugo, you mean you're leaving us?'

'Our time has end an we say adios. But for sure one day we break bread again.'

Ronnie scratched his five-day old stubble.

'You're right Hugo. It's all been spoken and decided. Our time together was destined to be a short, but memorable one, but I'm gonna be sad when we say our farewells all the same.'

Hugo turned around with a neat one-legged swivel. He tapped Ronnie on the chest with his crutch.

'Si, of course, this natural no? Come, cervaza time.'

Twenty minutes later we returned to the car laden down with several burritos, some tacos and a crate of Sol beer. Ronnie and I even purchased a couple of straw cowboy hats to protect our bonces from the sun's powerful rays.

I put my new hat on and I immediately liked it, placing it a jaunty angle just like the Sundance Kid or Butch Cassidy, or maybe just some stupid-gringo on holiday in Mexico for the very first time. Shit, it wasn't even eight o'clock, but I cracked open a cold beer and felt powerful.

We drove out of the frontier town and along another winding jungle road headed north. The utter remoteness of the scene induced an acute sense of anxiety. Not a soul knew of our whereabouts. What if Hugo planned to murder us for our money, slit our throats, and bury us in the heart of the forgotten Mayan jungle? I swigged beer and mulled it over. Anything was possible in this world. I studied Hugo. He smiled happily, his gold and ruby encrusted molars glinting in the misty morning sunshine. What was I thinking of? Old Hugo, murder me and Ronnie, was I nuts?

Ronnie turned the battered Volks down a desolate dirt track and along a steep and bumpy descent. All around was jungle, but as if by magic, a clearing appeared and several ancient structures hoved into view. It was awe-inspiring. Right there in the middle of impenetrable jungle was a lost Central American city, just like the ones I'd read and dreamed about as a child.

Several pyramids towered out of the jungle. Mist swirled around crumbling walls and temples, rays of sunshine piercing the canopy like laser beams. There was nobody around and the place had an eerie, ghostly quality. Ronnie stopped the Volks and took it all in. Hesus, the silent one, had arisen from the dead and stared out of the car window, his sad black eyes infused with a portentous intensity, and even Hugo let out a low whistle of impressed amazement.

I stepped out of the car. What had happened here? Why had the great city been abandoned all those centuries ago? Some of the largest and most densely populated cities the world had ever known had simply been deserted and left to disappear back into the jungle. In the dusty world of academia the historians and archaeologists thought they knew, but did they? I'd read of various explanations and logical proposals and wasn't convinced. Not even Spengler's words rang true. It was as big a mystery as the extinction of the dinosaurs.

Following Hugo, we marched towards a great pyramid

and climbed a series of stone steps until we reached the top. From this pinnacle a three hundred and sixty degrees panorama presented itself before our freaked optics.

We sat at the top of the pyramid and drunk our beers. I tried to imagine a vibrant and bustling city of several hundred thousand souls. I was aware of the violent aspects of Mayan history, the human and animal sacrifices and endless tribal wars, but in many ways they were much like us. They went to work, got drunk, high, fucked, procreated, lived and died. And then they just disappeared.

'This place has a strange atmosphere, don't you think?' said Ronnie, interrupting my ruminations.

Ronnie was right, an odd vibe permeated the scene, a sacred otherworldly aura. The same feeling you get when you walk into a ruined castle or monastery, or even a great cathedral. It's like you can feel something of the dramatic events that once occurred, the souls of the dead perhaps...

'Yeah, it's a got a spooky vibe, a weirdie aura, like maybe it should've been left to disappear into the jungle and take its secrets away with it forever.'

Hugo guided us to the entrance of a tunnel that led into the heart of the largest pyramid. It was dark and damp inside, with the daylight obliterated just feet away from the entrance. Hugo led the way, a cigarette lighter held high above his head, creating flickering shadows. We began a steep descent. The sound of our feet and breathing were the only noises, those and the occasional drip drip of invisible water. Then the tunnel widened and we entered a large chamber, the inner sanctum.

'Here is, here!' cried Hugo jubilantly.

We gathered around our one-legged friend and peered into the flickering light.

'Is Jade Jaguar throne, dis Maya royalty, Kings an Queens of old Bahlam Kin, an mia ancestor.'

I pulled out my lighter, to add a little more illumination. And lo and behold, there at the back of the room was a huge throne made of jade stone fashioned in the shape of a jaguar.

'Mother fucker,' said Ronnie.

How the throne was there after all this time was beyond me, but there it was. I pictured a Mayan king ordering another round of sacrifices or wondering which mistress would accompany him to the royal boudoir for a night of passion, Mayan style.

We re-emerged from the sultry confines of the mystery pyramid and out into a stinking hot twenty-first century sunshine jungle day.

'So where to now amigo, what's our next move?' said Ronnie.

'Si joo follow Hugo?'

'Follow you?'

Hugo hopped down from the last step of the ancient pyramid and walked back to the Volks.

'Si.'

Once again we found ourselves driving along deserted jungle tracks, the enigmatic Hesus at the wheel, until Hugo called a halt to proceedings. I peered out the window, nothing but jungle. The sinister thought that Hugo might just turn out to be a robbing murderer after all skimmed across the endless savannah of my paranoid mind.

'Come we go, joo see some beautiful amigos,' said Hugo, the look of a cold-hearted assassin flashing in his tantalising brown eyes.

We made our way single-file along a well-defined jungle path. The thunderous sound of rushing water was everywhere amidst lush palms, moss-clad tree trunks, vines, and the odd astonishing flower.

And there it was, several torrents tumbling out of a clear circle of azure, thrashing foam plunging hundreds of feet into a crystal pool. Hugo pulled out the jale. We all took a toot, even Hesus.

'Is bess waterfall Mexico an secret, no touristo, an if joo wan joo can behind.

'Go behind the waterfall?'

'Si, joo swims lagoon, is cave behind falls, is good thing no?'

'Is it safe?' I said.

Hugo nodded sagely.

'Si, jus no swim close, otherwise joo suck under, an possible you die.'

'Is possible I die?'

Ronnie stripped off.

'Come on what're ya waiting for? I've never sat behind a waterfall before, let's go.'

I eyeballed the waterfall. Fuck it, I had to stop thinking negative thoughts all the time. All I had to do was swim across a lagoon, easy. Hugo read my mind.

'Swim leff of pool Josep, an joo safe.'

'Any sharks in there?'

'No, ba maybe alligator.'

Ronnie had already made his way down, crashing through the undergrowth.

'Hey, wait for me.' I yelled, as I followed gingerly in pursuit, my balls and cock swinging free and easy in the dappled sunlight.

At the edge of the pool Ronnie and I stopped to consider a plan of action. The roar of the falls was deafening.

'Hugo said stick to the left.'

'Yes, that's right, that's right, that way we won't be dragged under.'

'Okay, you go first and I'll follow.'

Ronnie hesitated, and for one startling millisecond a flash of doubt appeared in his supremely confident expression, but that didn't last.

'Let's boogie.' he roared, and dived into the pool.

I gazed at his entry point. Some bubbles appeared and

then nothing. A few eternal seconds went by. The sheer size of the waterfall induced panic overload. Maybe the dynamics of the undertow were so powerful the forces had sucked Ronnie under, even from this distance.

I looked up to Hugo. He smiled and waved his crutch, oblivious to any impending tragedy. I peered into the inviting waters. I'd have to dive in and save my friend. I was scared, really scared, but there was no other option. I sucked in a lungful of air and was just about to dive, when a sudden movement caught my eye. My heart did a somersault. It was Ronnie, dragging himself bodily onto a green rock on the far side of the blue pool.

I cupped my hands together and yelled across the divide. Ronnie smiled. I don't think he was able to hear me. He waved and beckoned me over. It was now or never. I hit the water hard and went under. I opened my eyes. The water was translucent and grainy fishes, sharks, and crocodiles swum before my eyes.

Undeterred by my over active imagination, I rose to the surface and swum forward with powerful strokes. There was little or no undertow and it wasn't long before I reached Ronnie. We walked along a slippery path that wound its way behind the falls, where a recess had been carved into the rock by unknown hands. We found a stone ledge and gazed at the thunderous sheet of water.

'Look at that shit. What'd ya think, instant death if you stepped into it?' said Ronnie.

'Fuck yeah, total wipe-out.'

After a few minutes of sitting on the cold ledge in our birthday suits, admiring the falls and reflecting on stuff, Ronnie stood up and paced the damp recess, spray from the falls glistening upon his athletic body.

'This is it, I'm never going home.'

'You what?'

'I'm gonna stay on here for years, never go back to London, fuck London and England.'

'But how? We don't speak Spanish and we're not allowed to work here.'

Ronnie sat down beside me, so he didn't have to roar.

'There are other ways of living, other means of survival. We'll find a remote stretch of coast, build a hut to live in, fish the sea, grow organic food, write poetry and cultivate a herb garden.'

'Shit, you sound like an old hippy.'

'Maybe they had the right idea. Look at modern life, it brutalises and then clinically destroys. And everybody unhappy, stuck in the rat race, wage slaves, suckers one and all. What do they do, I mean look at how they live? Commuting far underground in conditions not fit for livestock or stuck in endless traffic. Imprisoned in sweaty offices breathing recycled air, wired up to computers, staring at screens, surfing the web, pissing their time away on social networks, pawns for the marketing men and advertisers, consuming mountains of shit they don't and will never need. The tide is turning brother.'

'And just what direction is the tide turning?'

'In the direction of absolute freedom. It's time to switch off the computers, disconnection is imminent.'

'Disconnection is imminent?'

'I'm no longer prepared to be a pawn in their sick game. I'm gonna return to the land and the earth, where my forefathers came from. All that electronic gadgetry we're supposed to own - it means zero to me. I'll kiss goodbye to all that shit - live the simple life and choose my own way, with no one telling me what to do and when to do it. I'll be free brother.'

Ronnie folded his arms across his skinny chest, craned his neck forward, and peered into the falls.

'One thing is certain, I'm never going home again, and

you're either with me or against me.'

And what about me, did I want to go home? Did I want to disconnect? Maybe Ronnie was right, maybe we could survive in Mexico, maybe we could live off the fat of the land. Maybe we could survive without technology. Maybe we could.

'I'm with ya.'

Ronnie placed a wet arm around my shoulder and kissed my forehead.

'We're with each other, come on let's get back and say our farewells to Hugo.'

We swam back across the lagoon laughing and joking all the way, and scampered up the jungle path and into our clothes. Hugo was there, waiting patiently.

'Is good no?'

'Out of this world Hugo my friend,' said Ronnie.

Back in the Volks, Hugo handed over a piece of paper.

'We leave joo Bin Kahlam amigos. Joo wan beach, si?'

We nodded sadly, bereft that our time with Hugo was almost at an end.

'Here directions to beautiful beach, plenty senoritas, plenty sunshine, plenty cerveza, marijuana, plenty everything. You catch bus I tell, six hour, maybe more.'

Ronnie studied the note.

'La Playa de los Muertos?'

'Si,' replied Hugo. 'Is mean Beach of de Dead in ingles.'

'Beach of the Dead, I like the sound of that name,' said Ronnie. 'So out of curiosity, tell me one thing: why is it called that Hugo?'

'Mia, a, why is sol, sol?'

Ronnie smirked.

'Great fucking answer Hugo, pure Zen, okay we follow your advice and go to the beautiful Beach of the Dead.'

At the town in the middle of nowhere, Hugo and Hesus dropped us at the bus station and bid their final farewells. Before we knew it they were gone, the car leaving a trail of dusty clouds in its wake, before negotiating a bend in the road and disappearing out of sight.

-29-

I slept eight hours straight. Ronnie woke me when it was time to get off. Once we collected our baggage the bus left us standing at the end of a small winding lane that ran away like a bitumen snake before disappearing into the ether.

Ronnie peered into the darkness.

'It's a 5K trek to La Playa de los Muertos. No buses along this route and at this time of night we're unlikely to get a taxi. You up for it?'

I slung my backpack over my shoulder.

'Let's go.'

It was a long and lonesome walk along that dusty track way down south. There was no sign of human habitation and zero lighting. We walked in silence, the sound of a million insects our only company, and every now and then the shriek of an unknown animal piercing the night like a vampire.

We walked and walked, hardly talking, just intent on making it to our destination. A soothing sea breeze feathered our weary brows as thunder rumbled in the distance.

'Can you hear that?'

'Hear what?' replied Ronnie.

'The sound of the ocean.'

It seemed like we walked forever, until a battered green road sign with an arrow pointing towards our intended destination loomed around the next bend in the road. Then glowing yellow lights, the first sign of human habitation since leaving the bus appeared as the ocean's roar increased in volume. The next thing we were walking on the soft sands of an empty beach, dark and eerily quiet.

We traipsed across the sand for a mile or so. In the gloom

all we could make out was a succession of wooden beach huts, guesthouses, and other ramshackle establishments. A row of empty hammocks hung forlornly outside one of the huts. A sign was out front, Penelope's Restaurant and Cabana, but there was no one around, no lights, no nothing, not a sound.

'Let's plot up here for the night,' said Ronnie.

We chucked our backpacks to the sandy floor and crawled inside a hammock each. The roar of the ocean was all around, a perpetual, comforting sound and up above a cluster of wealthy stars surrounded a lucky silver moon. I wrapped myself in a hammock cocoon style and swung gently to and fro.

'Well, we made it,' I said.

'Yep,' said Ronnie.

-30-

A pretty Indian girl spoke exclusively in Spanish, keen brown eyes, naturally inquisitive. She held a notepad, pointed to the hammocks, and continued speaking in Spanish, not a word of which I understood.

'No comprehendie,' I said, and closed my eyes.

The girl poked me in the ribs with her pen. I opened my eyes.

'What?'

'Ingles?'

'Si.'

'Si, hammackos, di nero, pay!'

I handed over a slim wad of pesos. The girl counted the cash, furrowed her brow, and handed most of them back. I counted the notes. The girl had charged the equivalent of $1.50 for a night's kip. Bargain.

'What's your name, nombre?' I pointed to myself, 'Joseph.'

'Yosep,' the girl replied thoughtfully. 'Soy Juanita.'

Ronnie remained asleep, safely ensconced inside his yellow hammock, snoring peacefully. The hammocks were situated at the western end of a substantial beach and there, not more than a hundred yards away, was the Pacific Ocean, a series of blue-green rollers cascading towards shore, whereupon they broke out into tumultuous and roaring white surf.

'Surf's up,' I said softly.

Spread out in a classic curve, the beach was hemmed in at each end by towering jungle-clad cliffs. An unruly collection of wooden huts, restaurants, bars, and other low budget accommodation lined the beach. Here and there palm trees swayed and brightly painted fishing boats lay idly at the water's edge. There were few people around, a lone surfer, some scattered sun-worshippers, a handful of bathers splashing in the shallows.

As I took it all in Ronnie finally roused.

'Pretty cool, eh?' I said.

Ronnie ruffled his bed head and let out an extended yawn.

'I've got a good feeling about this place, you know, a good vibe. I reckon we'll stay here.'

Two men walked past, one black, one white, wearing nothing except a towel hung over a shoulder. They stopped not fifty yards from where we stood and began practicing yoga.

'Come on, let's explore the vicinity,' said Ronnie.

With that we headed off down the beach, taking everything in as we ambled along La Playa de los Muertos. We wandered to the far eastern end passing two or three tiny restaurants, several huts, and the odd beach bar.

'Man, this place is beat,' said Ronnie.

The far eastern reaches of sand were desolate, nothing aside from one defunct beach bar and a collection of derelict huts. We turned around and headed back the way we had come, strolling across the sand. The ocean roared, the surf pounded, and the Beach of the Dead felt like the place we were meant to be. The last hut and restaurant was Penelope's Cabana, the hammocks hanging on the veranda, Juanita waving and smiling. We carried on walking, our feet making patterns in the sand.

-31-

At the west end of the beach it was another story. There were more people for one thing, more energy and life. And the people were all nude. Ronnie and I glanced at each other.

'What the fuck?' I said.

'Jesus, check it out, tits to the left of us, bushes to the right, I think I've died and gone to heaven.'

Everywhere naked men and women sunned themselves on the sands and paddled in the shallows. To our left were a group of Mexican girls, laughing, talking, carefree. Thighs met derrieres, the quivering movements the skin made in those regions were arousing and erotic. Wearing dark sunglasses I blatantly ogled the women. Those supple bodies were poetry in motion, a spectacle of raw beauty to rouse the most dormant of libidos. Ronnie was talking.

'I knew we could rely on old Hugo to guide us to our very own Shangri-la. Fuck, maybe we should go commando as well?'

I looked at us standing there, the only ones with any clothes on.

'You think we should?'

Ronnie whipped off his shorts. 'When in Rome,' he said, before running off and jumping into the ocean.

I took off my shades and kicked off my plimsolls. Then I glanced around. Everyone on the beach was looking at me or so I thought. Fuck it. I peeled off my shorts, ran down the beach, and dived straight into the foam. Then Ronnie was there by my side. We faced the shore and bobbed up and down in the waves, treading water.

'It feels good doesn't it?'

'Yeah, only way to swim.'

Ronnie gazed toward the shore. 'Man, I hope I get to shag a few of those lovely ladies,' he said, as a huge roller lifted us a good ten feet higher.

'So do I,' I said as the breaker sucked us down again.

We remained floating in the sea, buoyed by the power of the surf. Ronnie pointed towards some jungle-clad cliff tops.

'Look there, high up on the cliff. Looks like some sort of huts.'

'That would be a great place to live.'

Once out of the water we strolled to the foot of the nearest cliff, cutting through a group of nudists, and copping decent views of breasts and bushes along the way, and the odd flaccid cock.

An indistinct path, two-thirds hidden by encroaching jungle, wound its way upwards in meandering zigzag fashion. We started up the path, climbing higher and higher, the views expanding as we ascended. We came to a recess in the cliff where two huts and a lean-to were situated. The huts were in an advanced state of dilapidation.

The cliff ledge was around a hundred foot long and twenty or thirty feet deep. We inspected the gloomy interiors of the huts. There was nothing inside, except dusty old shelves, the odd wooden beer crate, and scattered rags.

'Whoever lived up here must be long departed,' said Ronnie.

I kicked one of the beer crates. A cloud of dust rose into the air.

'Doesn't look like anyone's lived here for years.'

'What do ya think then?'

'What d'ya mean?'

'Seems like a good place to plot up, just check out those views.'

I turned around. The sky and ocean spread out endlessly, one a sparkling diamond encrusted vision, the other a Virgin Mary blue.

'Better than any penthouse suite or five star luxury hotel.'

'And I've thought of a name for the place.'

'Such as?'

'The Starlight Hotel.'

'I like it, and I've thought of a name for our huts.'

'Give it to me.'

'The Huts of the Lost Elation.'

'That's right, that's the name, that's the name.'

'I've always been in search of the lost elation, like trying to re-capture that feeling you had when you were young, a moment in time. Like lost innocence or when everything was new, like a never-ending series of life firsts.'

Ronnie clapped his hands and let out a whoop of joy.

'And where better to find it than at the Beach of the Dead? Better still it's all free and that is now a very important factor.'

'Why's that?'

'Oh shit, I was gonna tell you later on this evening over dinner or something, but you might as well...'

'Might as well what?'

'Know about the money situation amigo.'

'The money situation?'

'I'm not sure how, but we've somehow spent over two thirds of what we originally started out with.'

'How, I mean when or what...'

Ronnie sat on one of the busted beer crates.

'Not sure, I've gone over our expenditure in detail and there's seems to be a good two thou missing.'

I found a crate in the doorway of one of the huts and sat down.

'Fuck.'

'Yeah fuck indeed. All I can think is that a lovely La Merced whore dipped into one of our money belts while we were otherwise engaged.'

'How much we got left?'

'A monkey.'

'A monkey?'

'Yep, five hundred fucking miserable dollars, barely last a month.'

I gazed out of the crumbling Robinson Crusoe jungle hut. The ocean swayed in the sunlight like a carpet of precious jewels, and here and there a pelican drifted past. Since escaping London, money or lack of it had been the least of my worries. We'd set out with enough funds to last months on the road, but just days into our big trip and it was almost all gone.

'So what's our next move?'

'It's not all bad. We've still got our onward flight connections and our valid work visas for Oz. We go on an ultra economy drive. We set up home here on the cliff and sell all our valuables.'

'Even our music?'

'Everything.'

-32-

The next day we rose early, just after sunrise, to the cacophonous sounds of seagulls and pelicans. We'd spent the night on the cliff top, and despite a lack of beds and amenities the lofty location had provided a remarkably pleasant night's kip. Cool sea breezes, peaceful tranquility, and a noticeable lack of mosquitoes. I gazed down on the yellow beach and blue ocean. Close to shore a pod of dolphins rode the crest of a perfect roller like superstar surfers.

'Dolphins!'

Ronnie rushed to join me.

'Ha, well, what d'ya know?'

We watched the dolphins. They were in total control, merely toying with the forces of the ocean, complete mastery of their chosen environment. It was a majestic display, but Ronnie was keen to get things moving and possessed super-motivation. He paced the ledge pointing and gesticulating, the personification of dynamism.

'Yep, we've got work to do. Get the huts in order, build beds, windows, make the place a home from home.'

I gave the crumbling huts and al fresco surroundings a cursory glance.

'What about taking a dump?'

'We can piss into the wind, but aside from emergencies, shits will be deposited in the rest rooms of the nearest bar.'

'And what about washing and bathing?'

Ronnie pointed towards the ocean.

'In the drink with a bar of soap. We'll be the cleanest freaks around, clean arseholes, clean cocks, clean everything. Now come on, let's head into town, see if we can offload all our useless electronic crap and get our hands on some basic essentials and fundamentals.'

It was then that I remembered an important detail. I grabbed Ronnie by the shoulder.

'There's just one more thing.'

'Shoot.'

I placed my hands behind my back and strutted the ledge Napoleon style.

'As you are aware I'm a geezer who likes a cold beer or two at lunchtime and six or eight in the evening. Also, when hung over, I'm often in the need of copious amounts of iced water or soft drinks for re-hydration purposes.'

'Yeah and?'

I swept a languid arm in the general direction of the shacks. 'And, I do not see any sign of refrigeration in this here Starlight Hotel. And let me tell you there is nothing worse in this world than tepid or luke warm refreshments, I mean a man could...'

Ronnie cut me short.

'Shut up, I've already considered that. Once in town, we get our hands on an ice-chest. There's bound to be an ice-man servicing the local bars and restaurants, all we'll have to do is stock up on ice every day or so.'

Immediately I pictured the scene. Me, lying in a hammock, reaching out for a bottle of cold beer floating in melting ice, just as a blood-red Mexican sun sank into the ocean after another hard day in paradise.

'Sounds good to me amigo,' I said dreamily.

Ronnie descended the jungle path.

'Of course it sounds good, now let's hit Penelope's and get some breakfast.'

-33-

Penelope's was deserted, the Mary Celeste of cabanas. On seeing us Juanita smiled and picked up her little notepad and pen. We found a table with outstanding sea views and plumped ourselves down in rickety wooden chairs. Immediately Juanita was on the case, jabbering away in Spanish, and handing over a couple of laminated menus. Ronnie waved them away.

'No need for that shit senorita, we would like dos burrito deluxes.'

'Que?'

Ronnie grabbed one of the menus and explained what he wanted by pointing at the list of burritos. Juanita wrote down something in her notepad. Then she turned to me.

'And I'll have the same.'

While we waited for our breakfast Ronnie outlined the plans.

'We need to find a local market, set up a temporary stall, offload our useless consumer rubbish and stock up with all the shit we need to build our huts.'

'Such as?'

'Er, you know, nails, wood, furniture, blankets, curtains, miscellaneous tools, shit like that.'

'And an ice chest.'

'Exacto mundo.'

Twenty minutes later Juanita reappeared with our breakfast. The burritos were suitably huge and delicious.

'Gracias,' said Ronnie. 'Now, can I ask you a question?'

'Si.'

Ronnie raised the tone of his voice several decibels. 'Is – there – a – local mar-ka-et – nearby?'

And it was at exactly that point that a voice spoke out, the voice of an American.

'You guys wanna know the loc-ation of the nearest mar-ket?'

We spun around. Standing before us was a sun-baked, prematurely aged, Gandalf look-alike. The stranger was barefoot and dressed in wizard or shaman robes. He held a huge wooden staff in one hand and what looked like a telescope in the other. He had long, lank, greasy brown locks, almost colourless grey eyes, and a hooked nose. However, the most startling aspect of his eccentric appearance was his facial hair or lack of, one side of his boat race being entirely covered in substantial brown beard, the other clean shaven and immaculate.

'Hello,' I said.

'Hi,' said the stranger.

'So where is the nearest market?' asked Ronnie.

The wizard spoke in measured and listless tones. 'There's one in town and you're in luck coz today is market day. In fact, I'm going. If you want, you can come along with me.'

'What time?'

'Er, in about an hour man.'

'Where d'ya wanna meet?'

'I'll meet you here, at Penelope's.'

'Okay, see ya in an hour.'

'Yeah, yeah, great, hey wanna take a peep at my universal kaleidoscope?'

'Groovy,' said Ronnie.

The stranger handed over the object. Ronnie held it to his eye for a few seconds, then handed it back.

'It's just a kaleidoscope.'

'To you maybe, but in fact the secrets of the universe are inside this chamber my friend, despite what the scientists might tell us.'

'Really,' I piped in, 'can I have a peep?'

The stranger handed over the instrument. I held it to my eye. Ronnie was right. It was just a kaleidoscope, the patterns swirling and mesmerising. I handed it back.

'I think you could be right,' I lied.

'You, my friend, have cosmic vision.'

And with that enigmatic comment he was off, shambling away down the Beach of the Dead.

'What the fuck was that about?' I said, with the odd stranger out of earshot.

Ronnie leaned back in his chair.

'That, amigo, was the Kaleidoscope Kid.'

34

I followed Ronnie and the freaky wizard along a winding jungle road. It was a five kilometre walk into town and I sweated each and every step of the way. The Kaleidoscope Kid said very little and whenever we fired a question at him, the only response we got was this:

'There are more questions than answers my friends and whatever answers exist are contained within the universal kaleidoscope.'

'Whatever,' mumbled Ronnie.

Every so often the enigmatic and barmy wizard took a sip from a roughly hewn wooden cup.

'Wonder what he's drinking,' I said.

'Only one way to find out. Hey geezer, what's that you're drinking?'

On hearing these words, the wizard stopped in the middle of the road and lifted his dirty cup as if it were a sacred chalice.

'Contained within this receptacle is the elixir of life, the sacred medicine, the nectar of the Gods, manna from heaven.'

'You mean beer?' said Ronnie.

'Beer?' he said, 'is the work of Satan, the ruination of man and the originator of great stinks. No, contained within this ordinary cup is a beautiful concoction that enables an individual to experience the secrets of the universe, and be at one with God.'

Ronnie spoke out of the corner of his mouth.

'Can't get a straight answer out of this fruitcake.'

'I thought you said the secrets of the universe were contained within the kaleidoscope?' I said.

'They are, but you have to be under the influence of the sacred medicine to experience it. This explains why, when you peered into the chamber, all you saw were reflected patterns. Whereas when I look into it I experience eternity.'

'Bullshit,' said Ronnie.

'So what is in the cup?' I demanded

The wizard narrowed his eyes, until they were slits. Then he uttered one single word, low and mysterious.

'Peyote.'

Peyote, the sacred and powerful hallucinogenic native Indians had ingested during traditional religious rituals since the dawn of time. I'd also read Jack Kerouac describing its effects in his famous novel, *On the Road*.

'Peyote?'

'Yes, peyote my friends.'

'I've always wanted to try that shit,' I said.

'Yeah, so have I, where can we get hold of some?' asked Ronnie excitedly.

The wizard looked us up and down, before spinning around three or four times like a whirling dervish until he was nothing more than a blur. When he eventually stopped spinning, he closed his eyes and pointed his universal kaleidoscope at us.

'You, my friends, can obtain the elixir of life from my very self.'

'Now you're talking, how much?'

The wizard opened his eyes and stroked his cheek, on the bearded side only, before embarking on an impressive and poetic sales pitch.

'The effective dose for mescaline is around 300 to 500 milligrams, effects of which last ten to twelve hours. When combined with an appropriate setting the sacred medicine is powerful enough to trigger states of deep introspection and induce philosophical insights of a life-changing, metaphysical, or spiritual nature. If you're properly tuned in, I mean like in the correct transcendental zone these can be accompanied by rich visual or auditory effects and maybe, but highly unlikely resulting in a ghost dance.'

A ghost dance, what the fuck did digesting peyote have to do with a long forgotten movement of North American Plains Indians origin? Ronnie didn't seem to care.

'How much amigo?'

'Five bucks for a ten hour trip.'

Ronnie pulled out fifty dollars.

'I'll take ten trips.'

'Ten?' said the wizard, surprised.

'Yeah, ten.'

The wizard took the money and held out his hand.

'It's a deal.'

Ronnie shook hands with the dirty-robed one.

'Nice.'

35

The village market was small and colourful. The wizard gave us the low down. There was zero bureaucracy, no fees, no inspectors, no parasitic council employees or irritating jobsworths to contend with. Lay a blanket on the ground, display your wares to all and sundry, and get down to the ancient process of bartering. Once he'd explained the process of doing business the wizard left to do his weekly shopping, promising to meet us at Penelope's the next day and hand over the Peyote, in an informal ceremony he obliquely referred to as the Righteous Harmony Handover.

We laid out all our electronic shit on the ground, camcorders, cameras, mobile phones, MP3 players, etc. Everything we'd stolen at the airport in duty free, before boarding our plane to Mexico. Duty Free is a shoplifters paradise. The retailers and airport banking on few people risking their one holiday a year by getting caught thieving, only maintain a low-level security presence. For any experienced tea-leaf it's a light-fingered opportunity not to be missed.

Once the gear was set out we waited for the offers to come rolling in.

'When we take the peyote, we should find a deserted beach or uninhabited island. Somewhere we can't be disturbed, should intensify the experience, maybe even glimpse the secrets of the universe,' said Ronnie as we waited for customers.

'You sound like the Kaleidoscope Kid.'

'No, I'm serious. Don't want any distractions, not whilst under the power of the peyote. I've taken plenty of acid, but this feels different, more in tune with nature and so deserves a natural backdrop.'

'Yeah, somewhere nice and mellow.'

'Of course. Now you stay here and sell the goods, whilst I go round purchasing everything we need for our new home.'

'Our new home?'

'The Huts of the Lost Elation.'

While Ronnie embarked on his mission, I stood around and tried to sell stuff. The locals showed little interest in what I had to offer and the high level of indifference seemed important. I studied the goods. They were truly useless, but people in the West held the machines to be worth substantial amounts of money. Why was that? Why do people feel compelled to consume shit they don't actually need? Was it apathy, or the benign brainwashing of the masses by capitalist money-makers?

A couple of stultifying hours passed. Zero interest. I studied the other stalls, grocers, clothes, women's lingerie, fruit, vegetables, tacos, household goods, plenty of customers. I lowered the asking price of each item. I got bored. Then I espied a stall selling ice-cold beers. I strolled over, purchased a bottle of Dos Equis, supped it and felt better. A gang of Mayan boys appeared on the scene, teenagers, vibrant, constant chatter, a little annoying. They picked up the items and examined them carefully. I sucked on my beer and retained a visage of exterior cool.

A series of questions were fired at me in high-velocity Spanish. We bartered for the goods, me and the boys. I didn't understand a word. It didn't matter. I sold everything for less than $300. It wasn't much, but better than a poke in the eye. Then, Ronnie returned, eyes wide open.

'Mother, you got rid of the lot?'

I assumed a smug expression and produced a wad of pesos.

'Yep, sure did.'

'How much?'

'Er, $300.'

'$300, that shit was worth $1000, minimum!'

'Best offer all day.'

'No matter, it's better than a poke in the eye. Come on, I've brought everything we need for the huts, spent less than a hundred bucks, even got a truck to take all the stuff back to the beach, let's go'

'What did ya get?'

'All sorts, plus a dirt cheap gramophone.'

'A gramophone?'

'Complete with a stack of ancient 78's, for if music be the food of love, play on, give me excess of it...'

36

The truck driver was kind enough to drop us off right outside Penelope's and once unloaded we dragged the gear to the foot of the cliffs and the little overgrown path. As always Juanita stalked the shady veranda of Penelope's. She waved. The afternoon sun melted the distance between us. I was hot and thirsty. The thought of a cold beer crossed my mind, a cold, cold beer.

'Let's get a beer,' I said.

Ronnie eyeballed the jungle path rising upwards a good three hundred feet.

'Good idea.'

At Penelope's, Juanita was curious to know what we were doing. She inspected the stuff.

'Wha joo do?' she asked, as we supped our cold beers in the shade of the veranda. Ronnie pointed to the cliff top.

'We go live there, up there, we make casa up there.'

Juanita peered in the direction Ronnie was pointing.

'Ingles, loco, loco.'

'And we also need some beer and ice, you got any Juanita?'

'Si,' said Juanita wearily and traipsed off to the kitchen.

Once stocked up with plenty of ice and beer we said goodbye to Juanita and began the laborious process of lugging the gear up to the ledge. It took a number of sweaty trips, but eventually we had it all up there. Then we got to work, making the huts into something resembling a human dwelling.

We tore out the rotted and wrecked wood, fashioned beds from wooden pallets, nailed timber to cover holes and gaps in the creaking walls, and completed a general spring clean. We chopped down bundles of verdant palm fronds from the garden of jungle all around and re-thatched the roofs, replacing the dried and yellowed stalks, and making it as water-tight as possible. We fashioned tables and chairs out of wooden boxes, hung beads in the doorways, strung small mirrors for vanity purposes, dug shallow graves at the back of the huts and placed the polystyrene ice chests inside.

Next we built a sink and washing-up area, a wooden structure to hold a plastic bowl, and hang our cutlery and cooking pots on. After the discovery of some large stones and rocks we improvised a fire place, along with a small lean-to to store dry wood and kindling. Last but not least we dug a couple of organic grease-pits some way from the huts for disposal of waste material.

By sunset we were tired and weary, but almost finished. Ronnie gazed at our handiwork with immense satisfaction.

'All we gotta do is carve the signs.'

'The signs?'

Ronnie produced his rocket knife and picked up a leftover plank of wood.

'Yeah, we need signs, to let people know how to get here. I'm gonna carve a Starlight Hotel sign, place it halfway down the path there, pointing upwards. Also, we need a sign for our Lost Elation huts. Gonna call mine, Cool Breeze, what about you?'

'Shangri-La.'

'Like it, for that's exactly what this is. An earthly paradise, well as near as we're ever get to one anyhow.'

'Looks like this calls for a little celebration?'

'Fuck yeah. Let's raise a toast to our essence of cabin by the sea.'

I grabbed a couple of beers from the ice chests and we retreated to our hammocks and cracked open the bottles with our teeth.

'To the Starlight Hotel and the Huts of the Lost Elation, Cool Breeze and Shangri-La!' I declared.

'I'll second that emotion,' said Ronnie.

We sat in silence, as a blood-red sun dropped into the blue arms of the pacific, and the distant roar of the surf lulled us into a trance-like state. Everything was how it should or would ever be. Maybe idleness was the secret to contentment? Up there on that jungle cliff top we felt as content as we'd ever feel, like we didn't have to go anywhere else, like we could just stay there and live life to its ultimate conclusion. We drank the beers slowly as darkness enveloped the land like a crouching black jaguar.

'When we get the peyote off Kaleidoscope Kid, we should also inquire about getting our hands on some quality weed. Shouldn't be difficult, after all we are in Mexico,' said Ronnie, as he whittled away at his wooden sign.

I lay there swinging in my hammock with closed eyes. Ronnie's word filtered into my consciousness. I hadn't had a single joint since my arrival in Mexico and hadn't missed one. It might be that I'd never smoke again. It didn't seem to matter. Maybe I didn't need to take drugs, smoke, drink? Maybe it was possible to lead a drug and vice free life like a hermit or an ascetic monk, or mystical fellaheen or ancient Brahmin. Relinquish all desires and thou shalt be free...

'Be nice to smoke a good spliff just as the sun comes up,' said Ronnie, 'and when the sun goes down, and maybe a couple at lunch, and then there's moon gazing and star gazing, so maybe a couple at night before bed. And one before a swim and it's always nice to have a spliff with a beer...'

I opened my eyes.

'You know I don't miss any of it,' I said.

'Any of what?'

'London, the UK, clubbing, pills, coke, herb, boozers, Pearl's café, our old friends, none of it.'

Ronnie put his embryonic sign down and fetched a couple

more cold ones from one of the ice-chests. He handed over a bottle.

'I know what you mean. I don't miss any of it either, the drug dealing, the plastic gangsters and cardboard cut-outs. Manic city life, everyone driven slowly insane by their crazy commute and crazy jobs, and the overcrowding, the pollution. And pricks like Baloney and psychotic numpties like Eyes Down, even the piss shit weather. That's why I don't intend on going back. I'm gonna be on the road forever, following the sun, putting one mother-fucking foot in front of the other, always on the look-out for a new sensation...'

The sky was a deep purple and blinking stars flashed dim-ly. Then I saw it, the rising moon, pale blue, smiling down on me. I didn't like to say the words, but someone had to.

'I'm with ya on that one amigo, but the cold hard facts remain. We're fast running out of cash.'

'I know, I know, don't remind me, but something will turn up. Tomorrow we get the peyote from the Kaleidoscope Kid, go on a mission, find a deserted and isolated beach, wait to see what the peyote reveals. I mean, you never know, we might have an epiphany, an illumination, something leading to money.'

'What, like the revelation of buried treasure nearby?'

'Yeah, why not? I mean fuck it. They had pirates round these sides didn't they, buccaneers an shit?'

'Shit, yeah!'

37

The following day I rose late and stumbled out of bed and over to the doorway of my hut. Ronnie was awake, standing at the edge of the ledge, legs apart, arms either side of his head. For one chilling moment I thought he was going to jump. Hearing my movement, he turned around. He was holding a pair of binoculars and smiling.

'Hey, hey, forgot I had these, quality Leicas chored from duty free at Gatwick. Found them in the bottom of my backpack this morning.'

'Seen anything interesting?'

'Lots of birds, all different types.'

'Birds?'

Ronnie handed over the bins.

'Down on the beach amigo and I ain't talking seagulls.'

I grabbed the bins and zoned in. What a vision, cavorting on the beach, ten or twelve girls playing volleyball in the naturist style. I adjusted the focus on the powerful German lenses until total clarity was achieved. Shit, tits, bums, thighs, and cunts so close I could just reach out and touch them.

'Oi stop perving and check out my sign,' said Ronnie.

I zoned in on a deliciously pert derriere as it shimmied across the sand.

'Er, what sign?'

'The sign outside my hut.'

Swinging above the beaded doorway of Ronnie's hut was a wooden sign. I strolled over for a closer inspection. Ronnie had carved the words, Cool Breeze, into the wood and given it a burnt finish.

'How ya do that?'

'Rocket knife and Zippo. I'll do one for you if ya like.'

I eyeballed my hut. There could be no denying the fact it didn't look right without a sign. 'Na, don't worry, I'll carve one and personalise it myself.'

'Plus I finished the Starlight Hotel sign. Come on, nearly time to meet the Kaleidoscope Kid. I'll show you it on the way down and then we'll go on a reconnaissance mission to locate the perfect place to take the peyote.'

I plopped my straw cowboy hat and dark sunglasses on and followed Ronnie along the jungle path. Halfway down the track Ronnie held out an arm.

'What?' I whispered.

He held a finger to his lips. 'Shussh, check out that huge fucker!'

'Where?'

'Twelve o'clock, ten yards.'

I zoned in. There, perched atop an impressive sign that Ronnie had carved into the shape of a curvaceous and contented looking whale, was a giant green iguana. Aside from the occasional blink of a yellowed eye, the reptile was motionless.

'Man, that dude is just chilling out, warming up that cold blood of his.'

'He's seen us but doesn't care, totally oblivious, a cool customer.'

'What shall we call him?'

'Freddie.'

38

With an hour or so to kill before our planned meeting with the Kaleidoscope Kid we embarked on a mission to locate a truly tranquil setting, a beauty spot where we could drop the peyote and experience a hallucinogenic life first in splendid isolation. We headed to the furthest reaches of the west beach and clambered up the cliffs.

Pathless and rugged it was a mad scramble to reach the top of a series of jagged ridges. Eventually we came to a point where a glimpse of coastline hoved into view. From this vantage point a coastal panorama stretched endlessly into fuzzy horizons. And there it was, down below, an isolated cove, nothing there aside from nature, rocks, a tiny beach of white sands, huge swathes of sea kelp and the sparkling Pacific Ocean.

'That's the place, the ideal setting to experience the power of peyote,' cried Ronnie above the roar of a stiff sea breeze.

With the location sorted we made our way back down to La Playa de los Muertos and Penelope's Casa. As usual, Juanita was the only body inside the tiny restaurant.

'Burrito deluxe?' she said, her little notepad and pencil at the ready.

'Si, and dos cerveza.'

We ate our tasty burritos and sipped our beers. With lunch over the Kaleidoscope Kid was already half an hour late for the rendezvous. We waited patiently. The sun lowered in the sky. Juanita sat under the shade of the veranda and idly flicked through the pages of a graphic comic. Some chickens pecked the dusty ground beneath our feet, a fly buzzed. Ronnie brought up the subject of getting hold of some weed.

'Maybe ask Juanita.'

Ronnie called her over.

'Where can, donde est, weed, er cannabis, no some mari-ju-ana?'

'Joo wan marry-ju-wana?' Juanita mimicked.

'Si,' replied Ronnie.

Juanita rested a hand on Ronnie's shoulder and pointed down the beach.

'Si, si, joo go Miguel, si marry-ju-wana.'

Some way off an athletic, ginger-haired man practiced naked yoga on the sands.

'Him?' said Ronnie.

'Si, si.'

Ronnie handed me some money. 'Right go over an get the shit.'

I threw the money onto the table.

'Whaddya mean, go over an get the shit, what about you go over an get the shit?'

'You're joking ain't ya, cock an balls swinging free, fuck that.'

'Fuck what, it's just the human body. Same as mine and yours, what exactly is your problem?'

'Point of principle.'

'Point of principle?'

'Yeah, and there's only one acceptable course of action.'

'Meaning?'

'Ching Chang Walla, best o three.'

Seconds later we stood in the middle of Penelope's deserted restaurant, facing each other, fists clenched, in classic rock paper scissors mode. It had taken a while to explain the rules of the game to Juanita, but once she'd digested the basics, she was more than willing to act as referee.

She raised one arm and glared at us.

'Una dos, tres,' she cried, before lowering her arm.

Our arms shot out at exactly the same time, mine paper, Ronnie's rock. Ronnie smiled and raised one finger on his clenched fist.

'Done like a chicken in a bun.'

Juanita raised her arm.

'Una, dos, tres...'

Our arms shot out again. Mine scissors, Ronnie's rock.

'Mother!'

'Blunted, 2-0 sucker.'

The next round was mine to win or lose. Juanita dropped her arm. Mine paper, Ronnie rock.

'Pushing ya luck there geez,' said Ronnie, with a rueful shake of the head.

While I blew on my fingers for luck, Ronnie narrowed his eyes. It was now a game of bluff. Juanita called, our arms dropped and it was an exact replica of the previous round, mine paper, Ronnie rock. I did a little jig. It was now winner take all. We eyeballed each other, searching for signs of weakness. The permutations were limited, but at the same time endless. Juanita raised her arm.

'Una dos, tres!'

Ronnie hesitated, I hesitated, neither wanting to make the final mistake. Then our arms shot out simultaneously, mine scissors, Ronnie rock. Shit, five rocks in succession; you had to have balls of steel to pull that one off. Ronnie opened his fist and blew on his fingers. Then he waved in the general direction of Miguel, who was doing a cartwheel on the sand.

'Run along fucker.'

Defeated, I grabbed the money from the rickety table and headed to my fate.

'Fuck you,' I said over my shoulder.

I stomped over to the alleged Miguel in a huff. When I got there he was performing a handstand. I was eye-level with his knobbly sun-tanned knees, his crown jewels inches away from my visage. I lowered my gaze earthwards.

'Miguel?'

'Yah,' the man said in a strong German accent.

'I've been told you can get us some weed.'

At that Miguel flipped over into a standing position.

'For sure, you wan hash?'

I nodded and proffered the cash.

Miguel glanced warily from side to side and hastily grabbed the notes.

'How much you wan?'

'How much will that get?'

Miguel counted the notes, approximately ten dollars' worth. 'More than enough for you gringo.'

'Yeah?'

'Si, where you stay?'

I pointed to the huts. 'Up there.'

'Oh, so is you up there, I was a wonder. Okay, I get stuff and bring you this evening, is okay with you?'

The thought I was about to be ripped off flitted through my mind, but this guy was naked on a beach, in Mexico. If I was gonna get ripped off by a naked yogist then so be it.

'Fine with me, tonight yeah?'

'For sure gringo.'

-39-

Back at Penelope's Ronnie was engaged in a game of cards with Juanita. They were using one of the retro porno packs we'd purchased in Mexico City. As I sat down Juanita showed me her cards and giggled.

'Nice baps on the seven of diamonds,' I said.

'Si.'

'Did ya get the gear?' asked Ronnie, without averting his gaze from his hand.

I wouldn't mind, but they were only playing Snap.

'Yeah, Miguel's gonna bring it to us tonight.'

'Tonight?'

'To the huts.'

'How much?'

'Gave him all the money you gave me, about ten dollars.'

'You paid upfront?'

'Yeah.'

'Fuck, knocked twice in one day.'

'Whaddya mean?'

'Well look, KK ain't turned up, an Miguel has probably already smoked our ten dollars.'

'You think so; I mean ten dollars, not really worth knocking someone for such a small amount is it?'

'Fuck knows, but where is the wizard?'

'Snapper!' cried Juanita jubilantly.

Aside from refreshing dips in the ocean and a couple of obligatory tit patrols we stayed in Penelope's all afternoon, waiting for the Kaleidoscope Kid to show his face, but funnily enough he never did.

Around sunset, we bought some takeaway beers and

retreated to our huts in the hope that at least Miguel would be true to his word.

Fifteen minutes later we lay in our respective hammocks, watching the dramatic changing colours of the evening sky and wondering if naked yoga boy would indeed show.

'What time did he say he'd come?' said Ronnie.

'He didn't.'

'Fuck.'

We whiled away the hours idly doing nothing. When darkness fell I lit some candles and a small fire. There was no sign of Miguel.

'I can't believe someone would knock us for ten dollars, I mean how lame is that?' I said in the dancing candlelit shadows.

'You can go a long way on ten dollars round these sides and as everything is relative, ten dollars might as well be a hundred.'

'It's still a dog move.'

'You're right, it is a dog move, an when I see that cunt I'm gonna...'

Suddenly a crashing noise sounded from behind the huts, amongst the impenetrable jungle that covered every square inch of the cliffs.

'What the fuck was that?' hissed Ronnie.

'Shussh.'

'What the fuck is it?'

'A troop of monkeys?'

We remained silent and fearful as the crashing in the undergrowth grew louder. It sounded like a parade of elephants back there. Then we heard the voice.

'Gringos, gringos you there?'

Seconds later, and Miguel emerged from the shadows. He wasn't naked, but only a pair of battered shorts covered his modesty.

'How's it going?'

'Alright,' said Ronnie.

'Where the fuck did you come from?' I said.

Miguel casually waved an arm in the direction of the bluffs.

'From the other side.'

'Is that possible?'

'Anything's possible gringo, now who want this?'

Miguel held up a plastic bag containing a large amount of cannabis.

'Me,' said Ronnie, and stuck his head inside the bag and took a sniff. When his head reappeared he was grinning. 'Smells the bollocks.'

This cockney turn of phrase confused Miguel.

'Smells what?'

'I mean, it smells good, very, very good Miguel and plenty of it so thanks very much.'

'Is nothing, some of best smoke in Mexico is grown locally. Totally organic, so is not only good shit, but healthy environmentally friendly chemical-free shit as well.'

'Blinding,' said Ronnie, 'care to partake?'

At that Miguel produced a bamboo pipe from a pocket of his tattered and torn shorts.

'Just waiting for you ask, got papers?'

While Ronnie fetched the papers, I grabbed a cold beer from my ice-box.

'Beer?'

'Er, usually don't drink, but hey why not?'

I popped the cap and handed over the beer.

When Ronnie returned with the papers Miguel rolled a long weed joint and stuck it in the end of his bamboo pipe. He lit up and took the longest and deepest drag of a joint I'd ever seen. The end of the spliff gleamed orange and white as he exhaled an endless stream of grey smoke, before breaking out into the longest and most vocal bout of coughing and wheezing I'd ever heard. He thumped his bronzed chest a few times, before handing the pipe to Ronnie.

'Some cough you got there,' I said, as Ronnie took a noticeably less extended pull before handing the pipe to me.

'Si,' gasped Miguel.

I stuck the pipe into my mouth and took a drag. The effects of the weed hit instantly and it was strong, maybe too strong. I blinked my eyes and shakily handed the pipe back to Miguel, who stared at me in a weird fascinated sort of way.

'Good yah?'

'Yah,' I croaked.

We passed the pipe around several times and asked Miguel a few perfunctory questions about his life, but were unable to get a straight reply. When I asked him where he was from, he said he was from outer space.

Ronnie inquired after the Kaleidoscope Kid.

'Miguel, do you know the dude with half a beard, dresses like a wizard?'

'You mean Anton?'

'Sells peyote or allegedly does?'

'Yes, is Anton, what about him?'

'We gave him some money for peyote and arranged to meet at Penelope's today, but he failed to show.'

Miguel let go with another vocal bout of coughing.

'Don't worry,' he wheezed, 'you'll get your peyote for sure.'

'So why didn't he meet us?'

Miguel raised the pipe and took another monumental hit. He exhaled two streams of grey smoke through either nostril.

'Anton has no conception of time. To Anton, time is an entirely man-made abstraction of little or no importance but for sure you will get peyote, maybe not today, maybe not tomorrow, but one day.'

'Fabulous,' said Ronnie.

Miguel cocked his head to one side. 'Hey, can you hear that?'

'Hear what?'

'The wind?'

We listened carefully. A slight breeze was blowing from the west.

'Yeah, it's just the wind,' said Ronnie.

'But not just any wind, that wind was born far out at sea. At the moment it is merely a zephyr, but if my hunch is correct we could be in for a hurricane.'

'Really?' said Ronnie.

'Yes, why not, after all it is hurricane season, but you want to know something?'

We nodded.

'Although hurricanes are more destructive, zephyrs are infinitely more interesting.'

Ronnie raised the pipe and took a big hit. 'Why's that?'

Miguel stared for an inordinately long time, an unnervingly long time.

'A zephyr is a tiny wind current so small it can make one little leaf on a tree shake like it's in a tornado, while the other leaves around it remain perfectly calm.'

'Serious?'

'Serious gringos.'

After the fifth pipe I was fucked and Miguel's hacking cough freaked me out so much that I was convinced he was dying. On the sixth round I made my excuses and retired to my hammock. The sky was studded with a glittering array of astral objects. The eternal celestial wonders. I lay there stoned and star-gazing, star-gazing and stoned. I closed my eyes and countless visions paraded across my mind's eye. Then a voice. It was Miguel.

'Josef?'

'Yes.'

'Still stoned a?'

'Very.'

'Listen, good to meet you guys, but now I leave.'

I sat up in the hammock and shook Miguel's dirty hand.

'Good to meet you also.'

With that Miguel disappeared into the jungle behind the huts, crashing and thrashing all the way, until the commotion faded to nothing. Ronnie was standing on the ledge gazing at the night sky through the binoculars. He motioned for me to join him with a wave of an arm.

'Ere, come an have a look at this.'

'Look at what?'

Ronnie handed me the bins.

'The moon.'

I raised the lenses to my eyes and there it was in close-up, the silver-grey face of earth's natural satellite, the surface littered with a myriad of craters, hinting at a violent and turbulent geological past. It was fascinating.

'Breathtaking stars, the universe, the cosmos.' I said.

Ronnie nodded in agreement. 'Yeah the vastness of it all, the unknowing, the sheer size, the mad unbelievable timescales. Light reaching the naked eye from stars so far away, the light emitted hundreds of thousands of years ago. Makes you feel small doesn't it? What is man, but a slightly offensive, inconsequential, irrelevant speck on the surface of eternity?'

I scanned the firmament. Stars flashed madly. I didn't know their names or the whys and wherefores, but it hardly mattered.

"That's what I like about the cosmos. Nobody understands it; western science is unable to comprehend its meaning. They talk about black holes, string theory, expanding universes, big bangs, but in truth they have come to the edge of man's reason, and the eggheads still don't know shit.'

'That's right that's right. Why man was put on earth is a puzzle, a planet hidden away in some poky corner of a vastness nobody is able to calculate the size of is an eternal mystery of life. Here give me those bins.'

I handed Ronnie the binoculars and continued my philosophical ruminations.

'When you think about it, life is nuts. I don't understand how people can take the experience so seriously when at its core existence is absurd and unfathomable. How can they do that, take those stupid jobs so seriously, take buying consumer rubbish so seriously, take borders, wars, governments so seriously when nothing makes any sense?'

'Look, look, a shooting star!

40

I lay in a pool of my own sweat, nightmarish death visions swirling my sozzled cranium, while outside a white sun reached a brutal and electrifying zenith. Outside, the sound of the ocean, breakers pounding the shore, the sway of palm fronds above the roof of my tiny hut. I opened my eyes. The orange hammock swayed to and fro. I thought about zephyrs. Any gentle breeze, especially one from the west, named after the Greek God of the west wind. And the words of Miguel.

'A zephyr is a tiny wind current so small it can make one little leaf on a tree shake like it's in a tornado, while the other leaves around it remain perfectly calm.'

I dragged myself from the bed and stepped into the blinding white.

'And what if it was true?' I wondered aloud. The doubts were always there. I spoke my daily Blakean mantra.

'I must create my own system or be enslaved by another man's.'

After these meditations I threw myself into the hammock, grabbed the bins, and zoned in. The beach was deserted, devoid of nudists. Disappointed, I let the Leicas drop from my hand and onto the sandy floor of my natural balcony. I stared at the sky, a sea of azure, becoming mesmerised by all that blue, an ocean of blue. Then, for the first time that morning, I thought about Ronnie. I got up and checked his hut, hitting my head on the swinging Cool Breeze sign. The hut was deserted, empty and eerie, some dust particles swirling in sun-rays, a ghost hut.

Probably gone for a wander. I fell back into the hammock and resumed sky-gazing. A man could easily waste his entire life looking at a blue sky, at all that never-ending cerulean.

The hypnotic sounds of the ocean continued unabated. From somewhere a seagull cried. I closed my eyes.

An hour or so later I re-awakened and wiped away drools that had accumulated on my chin. I faced south and clocked the position of the sun, throbbing in the western half of the sky. Round three o'clock, I yawned, time for my afternoon little donkey.

I slipped into my jean cut offs, plopped my battered straw cowboy hat on, and made my way steadily down the dusty jungle path. Freddie the Iguana was perched on the Starlight Hotel sign, basking dreamily on another golden Southern Mexican afternoon. As I sauntered past I winked.

'Ready like Freddie?'

Freddie didn't move a muscle, didn't blink an eyelid, but he was ready.

As usual Penelope's was empty, the small wooden tables sandy and desolate, the grubby kitchen a paean to inactivity, black flies buzzing in a misshapen circle. Juanita sat with her back to the ocean, reminding me of Pocahontas waiting for Captain John or Dreyfus sitting on his sad rock on Devil's Island. I sat at the nearest sea facing table and didn't even look at a menu, and Juanita already knew the scene.

'Burrito deluxe?'

'Si.'

Then two European females walked in. Immediately I was entranced, Juanita forgotten. There it was right before my very eyes, the lost elation, a vision of feminine beauty I'd been searching for since day one of the great adventure. I found it difficult not to stare. No more than twenty, long black hair and the biggest blue eyes I'd ever seen, killer eyes.

41

I studied the European females, taking surreptitious glances, while waiting for my burrito. The other girl was taller than the girl with the black hair and blue eyes, but naturally blonde and green-eyed they contrasted nicely with each other. They could've easily been mistaken for sisters. In fact maybe they were sisters?

I overheard snippets of conversation in French. Ah two pretty French mademoiselles on a gap year to Central America. I thought of Brigitte Bardot, I thought of Paris, I thought of Byzantium, I thought of...

When Juanita re-appeared the French girls ordered coffee in English and my heart rejoiced. So they could speak the mother tongue. No communication barriers involved, all I had to do was introduce myself. And yet I couldn't think of any reason to talk to them. I had nothing to say.

I ate my burrito and gazed at the ocean. Juanita disappeared and re-appeared with the coffees. Then Ronnie walked in.

'Alright ladies,' he said.

'Hello,' said the girls.

Why couldn't I have thought of that? Ronnie was wearing his straw cowboy hat, shades, and a pair of dirty cargo shorts, the same ones he wore every day.

'Are you a cowboy?' asked the girl with the blue eyes.

'Yeah and I drink like one, so where are you lovely ladies from?'

'Switzerland.'

Ronnie pulled up a chair, 'Switzerland, one of my favourite countries in the whole wide world.'

One of his favourite countries? This was news to me.

'Have you been there?' said blue eyes.

'Nope, but always admired the neutrality aspect and the cuckoo clock. Beer anyone?'

'Isn't it a little early for beer?'

'Ladies it's never too early for beer, that's a well known fact. By the way has anyone told you how beautiful your eyes are? In fact they're so beautiful that after you're dead they should be taken from your sockets and displayed prominently in a museum for beautiful eyes.'

The girl blushed. Ronnie signaled to Juanita.

'Sexy senorita, cuatro Dos Equis por favor.'

Juanita was unimpressed.

'Stupido,' she muttered under her breath.

'By the way, what's your names, mine's Ronnie.'

'Sylvie,' said the blonde-haired girl.

'Netta,' said the black-haired girl.

Netta, Netta, Netta, what a wonderful name, beautiful, even though I didn't like it and thought it ugly.

Ronnie acknowledged me for the first time.

'Why are you there all alone, come over and introduce yourself otherwise people might think you're an anti-social.'

I stood up awkwardly and stumbled over, inexplicably flustered.

'Hi, my name's Joseph.'

'Hello,' said the girls brightly.

I blushed. It was Netta. She was surrounded by a strange aura, a radius of beauty that had an undeniable emotional effect upon me.

'Are you staying long here?' I asked hopefully.

'Just three days,' said Netta.

Three little days, 72 fleeting hours, 4320 minutes, and, and, and, well I couldn't do the math in my head, but probably a whole heap of lightning seconds as well.

There was Juanita with the beers. Ronnie raised his bottle.

'Here's to the start of a beautiful relationship that we will remember forever and forever more.'

Everyone raised their bottles.

'You are crazy boy,' said Sylvie.

'It's not me that's crazy Sylvie; it's the rest of the world that's crazy, just you remember that.'

Sylvie stopped giggling. 'Does rest of world include me?'

Ronnie looked Sylvie up and down, 'Maybe.'

'So you say I'm crazy?'

'Most of us are.'

'Okay crazy boy, how many sane people on earth?'

Ronnie took a hit from his beer and adjusted the angle of his cowboy hat until it entirely covered his eyes. 'Amongst all the billions currently residing on the planet?'

'Yes.'

'Three, maybe four if we're lucky.'

Sylvie turned to Netta. 'See, I tell you, he is crazy, crazy boy.'

'Anyway, none of that matters,' said Ronnie, flicking his hat back to its usual jaunty angle and standing up, 'come and have a look at our Starlight Hotel and the Huts of the Lost Elation?'

'The Huts of the Lost Elation?'

Ronnie dragged the girls out of Penelope's and pointed towards the cliff top.

'You see way up there, that's where we live.'

'You live up there?

'Yep, we sure do.'

Netta raised a hand to her head. 'We'd love to go up there.'

Sylvie nodded. 'Yes, you must take us there now Mister Cowboy.'

'All in good time girls, all in good time. First let's go for a swim.'

The girls eyeballed the roaring surf and magnificent rollers.

'Isn't it dangerous out there?' said Sylvie.

'Of course it is,' replied Ronnie, 'but that's what makes life interesting.'

42

I burst through the surface of the water with a propulsion of my upper body and opened my eyes. Yells and shrieks filled the air. Ronnie was in the midst of everything.

'Look out everyone, another wave's approaching, duck under and swim forward with me,' he cried.

On re-emerging we found ourselves beyond the surf in a gently rocking expanse of turquoise.

'This is beautiful,' said Netta.

Ronnie floated over to where I was treading water.

'Which one?'

'Which what?'

'Netta or Sylvie?'

I faced the two Swiss misses. Sylvie waved and Netta smiled and everything, life, the beach, even the universe was eternally golden.

'Er, Netta.'

'Good choice.'

We swam, floated, and paddled in the sea. We laughed, talked, asked questions, and got to know each other.

That evening Sylvie and Netta accompanied us to the Huts of the Lost Elation. The four of us watched another sunset sink away into nothing until just a few streaks of purple remained on the horizon. The girls swung to and fro in the hammocks. Ronnie and I sat on empty beer crates swigging cold beer and whenever possible, clandestinely discussing how we could seduce the girls, even get them to stay over for the night.

As darkness fell like a velvet curtain Netta noticed the ancient gramophone. She rolled out of the hammock and inspected the machine.

'Does this thing work?'

I pulled a stash of dusty records from within my hut.

'Yeah, just needs a wind-up.'

I wound the gramophone and played an album of ancient rumba instrumentals.

'Oh this is lovely,' said Netta, as she lay in the hammock and listened to the lilting music.

'What shall we do tonight, I think I would like to dance, do you like to dance?' said Sylvie.

'Dancing is a beautiful thing, if more people danced there would be less misery in the world,' I said.

'Yes, I want to dance tonight also,' said Netta.

'Let's go to the Spaceman Bar,' said Ronnie.

-43-

At ten all four of us were plotted up in the Spaceman Bar, a small shack situated at the west end of the beach. The crowd was a low-key affair, motley groups of travellers and drifters hanging around outside, while inside an overweight red-faced man with long grey-hair sat propped at the tiny bar. He was wearing faded blue espridrilles, a wrinkled, but expensive cream linen suit, and sunglasses after dark. The elder man smiled and put his arm on the shoulder of a diminutive Mexican drinking next to him. The Mexican had dark slicked-back hair and beady, furtive eyes. Immediately I didn't like the look of him. For one thing, he reminded me of Eyes-Down, the same shifty expression and air of unpredictably.

As we approached the older man addressed us directly.

'Hello boys, you're the boys I've been waiting to meet,' he gushed in clipped English public school tones reeking of old money and over-education.

Ronnie eyeballed the stranger.

'Yeah and why's that then geezer?'

The man stood up from his barstool and held out a blubbery hand.

'Hi my names Gabby, you're the chappies living up on the cliff top like regular troglodytes, yes?'

I wasn't sure about the troglodyte insinuation, but the guy reminded me of an ageing Orson Welles.

'Yeah, that's us.'

'I was just telling my friend Carlos here, how wonderful it is that people still possess the pioneer spirit, you know show a little imagination instead of following the herd. Now, you must let me buy you and your friends some drinks.'

'You must?'

'Yes, I must.'

'Okay.'

'Now what do you want, cocktails?

'We love cocktails.'

'Good, good, good, the frozen margaritas are highly recommended. And Ricardo here makes the finest strawberry daiquiri this side of Terra Del Fuego.'

When the drinks came instead of one each, there were two each. Our new friend explained his generosity.

'Come on young folk, the night is brand new and made for hedonists. Let us toast our new acquaintance.'

We chinked glasses.

'Now, what are you lovely people doing tomorrow night?'

'Not much, drinking beer, looking at the moon or some shit like that,' said Ronnie.

'That's all well and good, but I would like to invite you to a celebration at my hacienda.'

All four of us exchanged surprised looks and glances. We'd only just met this stranger and already he was buying us drinks and inviting us to parties. There had to be a catch. I studied him surreptitiously and for one eternal moment sensed an overwhelming sadness.

'And what are you celebrating Mr Gabby?' said Netta.

'What am I celebrating pretty mademoiselle? Only my fiftieth birthday and I'm inviting who the hell I like and I like you. For one thing you sure do look damned good. So is it a yes?'

'Where is your place, this hacienda?' asked Ronnie.

'Thirty minutes' drive from the beach. I'll pick you up here tomorrow night at ten. Be there or be square.'

Being no mugs me and Ronnie went to have a pow wow, but the girls answered without hesitation.

'We'd love to come.'

That's another thing I liked about Sylvie and Netta. They were up for a good time, not overly concerned with pitfalls or unseen dangers. There was no paranoia or unfounded fears and bizarre phobias that often disable others from enjoying life to the full. At that stage in life they could only see the good in people.

'Fantastic, you'll have a ball. There'll be free drink, food and a hired band. It should be a gas. And you're welcome to stay over. I'll drive you home the following morning or afternoon, or whatever. Okay, now enjoy yourselves on the eve of the night of nights.'

And with that Gabby, fat, old, red-faced and overweight, but strangely fascinating made as if to depart the scene. At the entrance to the bar he turned around.

'Hey, hey, but one thing you boys.'

'What?'

'I want a return invite.'

'A return invite to where?'

'To the Starlight Hotel of course.'

-44-

'Strange guy,' reflected Ronnie afterwards.

'How did he know about the Starlight Hotel?

'We told him didn't we?'

'Did we?'

'Yeah we did, anyway he seems okay. Hey girls, fancy another Margarita?'

'Yes, and then we dance?' said Netta.

We drank several cocktails and spoke to different groups of travellers, Europeans, Americans, Australians, South Africans, and Mexicans. The conversations were dull and stilted, the usual traveller bullshit. Soon we were huddled in our own little corner. Ronnie was trying hard to impress.

'Once our work is done here we're off to Honduras, Costa Rica, then down to Peru.'

'What work are you doing here?' said Sylvie.

'Joseph is a beach poet, the world's first. He's currently in the process of writing a hundred beach poems. As for me I'm a sculptor, engaged in sculpting the letters and codices of the ancient Aztec alphabet in sand.'

'That is crazy, but wonderful,' said Sylvie.

'Nothing crazy about it lady. It's been decided and spoken. After South America we hit Australia and go on a walkabout, from ocean to desert, mountain to hinterland, and then just carry on moving, continent by continent, composing sonnets, haikus, and sculpting whatever inspires.'

Netta slipped an arm in mine, her soft skin touching my skin, sensual and erotic.

'I like your friend, but think he a little crazy.'

Was Ronnie crazy? So far everything he said he was going

to do he had done. And write a hundred beach poems, why not?

'He's not crazy, he just has a lust for life.'

Outside a dozen or so young people were dancing in the sand. While Ronnie and Sylvie were busy ordering drinks at the bar, Netta grabbed me by the arm.

'Come on let's go outside.'

Netta held my hand and led the way. Within seconds I was dancing with her and she was holding me close, very, very close. She whispered into my ear.

'I love to dance. You can forget everything when you dance.'

Netta was right you could forget everything, all your troubles, sufferings, and life problems during a dance. When dancing you lived in the moment, like animals, like free spirits. To dance the night away seemed like a noble thing to do, like something all lovers should do, old or new. And so we danced and meandered further and further away from the bar, towards the sea, until we could see nothing but the night sky and stars, a luminous moon silver and beguiling. The sea breeze brushed our brows, soft, cool and luxuriant. I had to make a move.

'So what do you want out of life?' I cried above the music and muffled roar of the ocean.

Netta flung her head back. 'I want to be happy, that's all. I don't want to be rich or famous, just happy. And I don't want to be alone, oh God I'm drunk.'

She was drunk, I was drunk, the thought flashed through my mind. I should take her to the huts, to my bed in Shangri-la, otherwise all might be lost.

Then I heard the voice. It was Ronnie.

'Who wants to go skinny-dipping?'

'Yes let's, let's swim naked!' said Netta.

'Come on then let's go to the other end of the beach.'

Netta held out her hand. The touch was electric, her fingers clasped in mine, the flash of midnight blue from her eyes. And now it was a magic night where anything could happen, pre-ordained and pre-determined with the scent of flowers floating in the sultry Mexican air. Past Penelope's and the little jungle path that led to the Starlight Hotel, to a deserted stretch of beach. Aside from ghostly moonlight sending a shimmering moon glade across the sea everything was shrouded in primordial darkness, an impenetrable opaqueness through which nothing could be seen or discerned.

All four of us stood on the sand, and for a split second neither of us knew what to do or say.

'Well?' said Ronnie.

'Well, what?' I said.

It was left to the Swiss girls to make the decisive move. Netta stripped off, followed by Sylvie. Being a gentleman I pretended not to know where to look, but Ronnie blatantly ogled the girls.

Netta flicked her long black hair over her bared breasts and placed her hands either side of her shapely hips. 'What are you guys waiting for?'

Ronnie stripped off and so did I. Maybe it was a European thing, I mean the girls brazenness, but as soon as my shorts were off I dashed into the sea in a desperate attempt to hide the evidence of my reaction to seeing Netta in the flesh, fuck even Sylvie was fit. Ronnie followed, grabbing the girls by the hands and crashing into the sea.

I dived under and swum forward. The water caressed my nakedness. When I re-emerged, the others were some way away, Ronnie frolicking with Sylvie, Netta on her own, eyes searching for someone and that someone was me. I waved.

'Netta!'

She swam over. The time had come. I took her in my arms and kissed her. Our tongues entwined, twisting and turning. The water was only chest high and our wet bodies glistened in the moonlight.

The beach was deserted. Ronnie and Sylvie were nowhere to be seen. It was just me and Netta. We continued kissing. Netta wrapped her legs around my waist. My cock probed madly. Netta lowered herself. It was awkward, the ocean swell made footing difficult, but once in it was exhilarating, slippery, wet, sensual and sexy. Netta gasped and kissed me wildly

'Don't come inside.'

I grabbed her buttocks and sucked her wet, erect nipples. Then I pulled out and ejaculated into the murky oceanic depths, while Netta showered my neck with briny kisses. We wandered dazed to the beach, collapsing onto the gritty sand in a crumpled heap. The waves lapped at our feet and ankles, gently caressing them with foamy surf, our lips and goose-pimpled skin tasting salty and delicious. I looked into Netta's eyes. In the moonlight they revealed nothing and I would never be that young again. It was a bittersweet moment, transitory and filled with sadness, the full realisation that we are all born to die...

-45-

The hut was hot. Netta was beside me, sleeping peacefully. I remembered everything. She lay there naked. I studied the breasts and thighs. Dust particles swirled in streams of sunlight. I ran a hand across her brown stomach. Where was Ronnie or Sylvie? Where was I?

A half-finished joint lay in a clay ashtray that had the words Penelope's Cabana carved into the edge. Juanita had given it to me a few days before. I grabbed the joint, lit up, and took a deep drag. The first hit cleared my bleary head. I rose, pulled on my shorts, and stumbled from the hut.

Outside, the glaring white forced me to blink. The surf was up and a strong breeze was blowing.

'The peyote is here my friend,' said a voice.

I turned around, surprised. It was the Kaleidoscope Kid, swinging in Ronnie's hammock, looking cool, calm and collected.

'Where ya been, I mean why didn't you meet us at the agreed time and place?'

KK raised one hand red-Indian style. 'Where have I been, time place, place time, and where may I ask have you been?'

'What d'ya mean, where have I been?'

'Exactly, so why worry about time?'

'I'm not worried about time.'

'So why did you ask where I have been?'

It was true. I had inquired to his whereabouts so maybe he had a point.

'Okay, who cares where you've been.'

The Kaleidoscope Kid tossed a small plastic bag my way, which I caught mid-air.

'In that bag is enough Peyote for sixteen eight hour

experiences, mix two thimblefuls of the cacti with three parts water. After taking peyote you will never be the same again. Now we must shake.'

'Now we must what?'

'Shake,' said KK resolutely.

He shook my hand for an inordinately long time. Then his grip tightened unexpectedly before letting go. I grabbed the wrist of my crushed hand and shook it.

'Mother,' I said.

'The Righteous Harmony Handover has taken place and my work here is done. I bid you a fond adios.'

And with that he was gone, away down the path, dirty robes billowing behind him.

-46-

As soon as the Kaleidoscope Kid was out of sight I stashed the peyote into the horn of the gramophone and checked on Ronnie's hut. I was spaced and bumped my head on the swinging Cool Breeze sign.

'Fuck,' I said aloud. The hut was empty. A wave of anxiety. What if Ronnie and Sylvie had drowned in the Pacific? I gazed out to sea. The ocean was calm, the blue water sparkling madly, with no hint of tragedy.

Then the ring tone of a mobile phone sounded. The tinny electronic noise surprised me. I'd forgotten such technology existed. Netta was talking. I jumped into the hammock and listened in. The one-side convo was conducted mostly in French, with the odd English phrase and many a giggle. I figured it was Sylvie and she hadn't drowned after all. I swung in the hammock, heard my name mentioned, and felt freaky.

After a long time Netta emerged from the hut. I wondered if I would get to fuck her again.

'Good morning mademoiselle, please take a seat.'

'Buenas dias senor,' Netta said before lowering herself awkwardly into the hammock.

A prolonged silence followed. I didn't mind, sometimes it's good to just say nothing and be occupied by your own thoughts, in your own little world. Anyway I would've enjoyed staring at Netta for hours, admiring her beauty, trying to compose sonnets about her loveliness. Silence is golden.

Then I wondered if by saying nothing, Netta was conveying a clandestine message, regretting our impulsive and spontaneous actions of the night before? It was more than possible. Girls invest far greater emotional attachments to intimate experiences than men, even one night stands, and despite everything, we hardly knew each other. Well, it had happened and that was something that couldn't be denied. Sexy images flickered through the photographic department of my mind. I pulled up a wooden beer crate and plotted next to her.

'Do you have a mobile phone?'

'Oh yes of course. Sylvie just called.'

'Is Ronnie with her?'

'Yes, er no. I mean he was, but he has gone for a swim or something.'

We were silent again.

'It's beautiful up here,' said Netta.

'Do you want a drink or anything?'

Netta hung one bare leg over the side of the hammock, exposing an entire flank of tanned thigh. It turned me on just to look at her leg.

'No, no, I must leave soon. Sylvie and I will take trip into town.'

A trip into town? Any notion of a planned day of glorious sex in Shangri-La exploded into a million fragments before disappearing into a black vortex of nothingness.

'Shall I walk you down to the beach?'

'Yes please.'

We made our way along the path, always descending. Netta relaxed, becoming happy and childlike, pointing things out, picking flowers and laughing. Freddie was in his usual position, on top of the whale sign, unmoving. As Netta approached he cocked his head to one side and eyeballed her. It was the first time I'd seen him move. It appeared even the lizard wasn't insensitive to beauty.

On the beach Netta was keen to get away. I wasn't sure why or what it meant, if it meant anything, but it left me flat.

Maybe it was just one night of passion after all.

'Don't you want me to walk you back to your room?'

'No, of course not, it is just short way.'

'Okay, if you're sure.'

Netta flung her arms around my neck and gave me one last lingering kiss.

'I like you Joseph, I really do.'

'And we're still gonna meet tonight and go to the party?'

Netta was already walking away.

'Yes, yes of course and remember?'

'Remember what?'

'Tonight is our last night.'

Back at the huts, Ronnie remained on the missing list. I threw myself into my hammock and swung to and fro, recalling events from the previous night, picturing Netta in the sea, our bodies entwined in holy ocean communion, images of her body running over and over in my mind. Pretty soon my dick was iron. I pulled off my shorts and began stroking. With the sun on my face and a cool breeze feathering my cock and balls, it was sumptuously sensual, and I came within seconds, flicking the orgasmic juices into a bush.

Afterwards I listened to the sound of the ocean. In moments like these life was sweet. Then the sound of off-key singing could be heard.

'Love is in the air, everywhere I look around.'

It was Ronnie.

'How goes it amigo?' I called out.

Ronnie plopped down in his hammock.

'Man that was one wild shag, banged it six times.'

'Six times?'

'She was insatiable, a man-eater, wouldn't thought it to look at her.'

'Jesus.'

'But you know what?'

'What?'

'At first she wasn't up for it.'

'Wasn't up for it?'

'I mean, she wasn't prepared to go all the way.'

'She wasn't?'

'No, we were getting down to it, you know kissing, snogging, tits and bush out, a slow finger fuck when she freezes at the critical moment, just as I'm about to dip my wick.'

'Bummer in the summer.'

'And d'ya want to know what else?'

'What?'

'This may sound bad, but if she hadn't eventually bowed to my will, I sort of entertained the idea of raping her.'

'You what?'

'It was a question of morality, hers and mine. Up to that point she'd been more than a willing partner in our shared hanky panky endeavours. If she then decided, unilaterally, to rengage on what had up until that moment been an unspoken agreement to fuck each other's brains out, I figured it was an unacceptable infringement of my human rights.'

Ronnie told me all this in a purely matter of fact manner.

'What about Sylvie's human rights?'

'Again, purely a question of morality. Morality as we know it, is defined as a system or code that we humans use to differentiate between right and wrong. But who sets the boundaries? The way I look at it, I was morally justified and RIGHT to fuck Sylvie whether she wanted to be fucked or not.'

I glanced at Ronnie to see if he was smiling or on a wind up. His visage remained curiously impassive.

'You're joking right?'

'No.'

'But what about Sylvie's morals, what if they differed from your wonky ones?'

'They probably did, but that doesn't mean she was right.'

'Well, the way I look at it, she was well within her rights to refrain from full sexual intercourse if she so wished.'

'Yeah?'

'Yeah.'

'And what about my rights?'

'In that situation I think your rights would be rendered invalid on grounds of common decency alone, and also in the name of peace love and harmony.'

'Bullshit. Just because Sylvie's moral compass was out of kilter with mine, doesn't make her right.'

'Any court in the land would prove you wrong. You're acting on the assumption that an individual is justified to live by their own set of morals, no matter how reprehensible or odious to the general populace those morals may be.'

'That gets us back to who sets the boundaries.'

'I think you'll find those boundaries are set according to what, generally speaking, is in favour of the common good. Rape, as far as I'm aware, is in no way in favour of the common good. And, by ignoring those long-established moral codes, you are in effect being amoral.'

'You appear to be confused, maybe even brainwashed. What if by having my wicked way with Sylvie, I was acting in the name of the common good?'

'That's bollocks. No way were you acting in the name of the common good. In fact you were acting in an entirely selfish and self-satisfying manner, bordering on the criminally psychotic.'

'Yeah, but what if I was acting in the name of the common good?'

'But you weren't.'

'Again, we come right back to morals and who sets the boundaries.'

I looked at Ronnie like half his face was missing. 'You're nuts, and we're just going around in circles. Please cut the crap and tell me how this tricky conundrum was resolved, and how you did end up getting your nuts in consensually.'

'Get your nuts in consensually, that's a great phrase, I should write that down for future reference. Anyway it was the usual horseshit. Sylvie fed me some tired lines about how she didn't do this all the time. How she wasn't that type of girl, how she didn't want me to get the wrong idea, as if I had any ideas in the first place.'

'And?'

'And then she fucked my brains out and if anybody got raped, it was me. Anyway, what about you, get ya nuts in consensually?'

I tipped my straw hat low down onto my nose and emitted an artificial yawn.

'Hey, hey, happy days!'

And that was that, the weirdie convo was forgotten, as I suddenly remembered an important detail from earlier.

'And guess who came here this morning?'

'Who?'

'Only the Kaleidoscope Kid!'

'And he had the stuff?'

I let out another artificial yawn.

'Yep, stashed it in the gramophone horn.'

Ronnie leapt out of the hammock and over to the ancient musical machine. He pulled the bag out with a flourish.

'Knew we could trust that freak to come up with the goods.'

'Enough there for sixteen eight hour experiences.'

'Blinding, shall we do some now?'

I flipped the rim of my cowboy hat upwards.

'Are you loco? We've got Gabby's party later an fucked if I'm attending that one tripping outta my brain.'

Ronnie stroked his chin thoughtfully.

'Yeah, you're right, that could be a decidedly uncool freak out. Okay, we party tonight and when we're good and ready, take the peyote tomorrow.'

Ronnie raised the bag of cactus and kissed it.

'Hopefully this shit will come up with some beautiful illuminations and get rich quick schemes. For if it don't, we'll be begging on Bondi Beach within a fortnight.'

-48-

At nine Ronnie and I were in the Spaceman Bar, sat at a beachfront table, cold beers in hand. There was no sign of Gabby or the girls. Groups of hipsters wandered the peachy shadows, palms trees swayed, creaking and groaning ominously like whispers of long lost Mexican dreams, the souls of departed fishermen, sailors, and mermaids. Restaurant lights shimmered in the night, glowing yellow and homely, illuminating the darkness like fireflies. Enticing food smells drifted in the breezes, chilli and tacos, grilled seafood. Beach fires leapt and danced, one or two unidentified fellaheen crouched low, the snatched sound of a guitar and bongos, intermittent, sometimes loud then lost forever in the void.

We were excited, looking forward to the party and giving the girls a big send off on their last night at Playa de los Muertos.

'Do you think you'll see Sylvie again?' I said.

'Well, to get inside her knickers last night I pledged eternal devotion, told her she was the most beautiful girl in the world, but you know what holiday romances are like, in love one day, yesterday's newspaper the next.'

'But would you like to see her again?'

Ronnie took a reflective pull from his bottle of Dos Equis.

'I suppose, like if she invited me over to Switzerland for a dirty weekend I might consider it.'

I thought about why I was asking the questions. Maybe, deep down, I wanted to see Netta again. Yes, that was it, for despite everything I thought it would be sad if we never met again, even just once. I mean isn't that sad? Or maybe it was just me, maybe I was taking things out of context. It was just another holiday romance and how many brief encounters occur all over the world at any given time, a thousand, a million, a trillion? At the end of it all we were just two blobs, amongst seven billion blobs.

'You like Netta, don't ya?' said Ronnie.

'She's a nice girl.'

Ronnie slammed his bottle down on the table.

'And looky here, here are those nice girls.'

And there they were, Netta and Sylvie, strolling along the beach arm in arm with a ludicrously colourful Hawaiian-shirted Gabby, all smiles and happiness. Once more Netta was surrounded by a strange alluring aura, a throbbing corona of beauty. Ronnie tutted loudly.

'Don't just sit there gawking, get the drinks in, frozen margaritas all round.'

After handing out the drinks, I grabbed a chair and sat next to Netta. She gave my left knee a soft squeeze and winked. I smiled and blushed and felt an overwhelming urge to kiss her, but I never. It was a question of morals. Gabby held court.

'I can hardly believe it. Fifty tonight. Tonight I am fifty, five decades of life experienced. Now, I'm sure you young pups can't begin to contemplate such a great age, but believe me blink once and there you are.'

Netta smiled at Gabby and guided one of my hands to an inner thigh.

'So any advice for the young folks?' she asked.

I thought I was going to explode, the sensation of Netta's thigh having an instant and inexorable impact, the soft flesh tantalisingly warm to the touch.

'Advice, you mean like what to do with the rest of your life?'

Netta took hold of my hand and raised it higher. Shit, she was going commando.

The next thing I felt was pubic hair, soft and bristly.

'Yes, how shall we live Gabby, what should we do?'

Gabby raised his cocktail, downed the contents in an impressive swig, and eyeballed the table.

'Live everyday like it's a scene from a movie, like it might just be your last, like you were put on earth for just one day! Not practical of course, but if you grasp the spirit of the sentiment you'll get along just fine.'

Ronnie raised his glass.

'I'll drink to that and to Gabby's birthday.'

And with that declaration Netta brushed my hand away and we raised our glasses in a toast. We sang happy birthday and hip-hip hooray, but all I could think about was Netta's lack of underwear. I was on fire!

An hour later, fifty or so characters crammed into vehicles and drove convoy fashion towards Gabby's hacienda in the hills. Ronnie and I were squashed into the back of Gabby's jeep, Sylvie and Netta nestled snugly on our laps. Eventually the convoy drew into the gravelled drive of a gracious colonial villa.

Once inside, we gazed around the spacious interior of the hacienda wide-eyed. This was the sort of pad a young person dreamed of owning. A multitude of rooms, with a large veranda surrounded on all sides by lush tropical gardens, and from somewhere the gentle sound of running water. Music was playing, the sound of mariachis, the likes of which we hadn't heard since Vera Cruz. Strange people milled around.

Gabby led us into the main room, where all eyes were on us.

'Come on young hearts, let's crack open the champagne!'

'Check out the size of the drum, old Gabby must be loaded,' I said

Ronnie nudged me and raised a finger to his eyebrow.

'I'll wait till he's pissed and tap him for a hefty, never to be paid back loan.'

Within seconds we were holding a champagne flute each and standing on a vast terrace of Gabby's opulent hacienda. The evening was sultry and listless, filled with the scent of bougainvillea and frangipani. An impressive twelve strong group of flamboyant mariachis played loud rambunctious rumba, and beyond was an elegant swimming pool and fountain, the water features illuminated by underwater lighting standing out blue and white against a backdrop of velvet night. Floating in the swimming pool were several inflatables.

Gabby introduced us to most of the other guests, an odd collection of middle-aged ex-pats and locals. He kept telling everyone that he had found us at the local flea market, where he'd brought us from a mystery half Jewish Arab street vendor for sixty mules and a basket of mangos. The other guests seemed to find this fabrication hilarious.

'Sixty donkeys and a basket of mangos?' said Ronnie.

'Geezer's taking the piss.'

With the intros out of the way, Gabby disappeared and we were left to do as we pleased. We wandered from room to room. People talked and danced and the atmosphere was magical. We drank more champagne, we danced and sang as the night vowed to last forever. The band played on and on, lights blurred, and Gabby appeared with nothing on but a pair of swimming trunks, diving mask and snorkel.

'Pool party!' he cried above the babble of guests and mariachi music.

And with that order issued a large group descended to the pool, laughter and shrieks echoing into the night. Gabby jumped straight in with several fully dressed partygoers following suit. I found myself floating in an inflatable chair with Netta on my lap. We were spinning around and kissing. Ronnie and Sylvie floated past in another chair with champagne. Ronnie topped up our glasses as we floated by.

'Let's party till dawn,' he cried, as they and the chair floated to the other end of the pool.

The moonless night sky was studded with flashing stars and everything seemed just right. And then there was Netta, having the time of her life. She flung her arms around my neck.

'I'm so happy.'

And so was I. It was primordial happiness, fleeting and transient, yet fundamental to life itself, a reason to believe, a reason to procreate, so that others might also enjoy happiness that touched us that night, a moment to be savoured and never forgotten. I leaned over and whispered into Netta's ear.: 'I love you.'

Netta pulled away, her eyes bright and boozy, filled with electric energy.

'You love me?'

I blushed and felt silly like I'd stepped over some acceptable boundary, and ruined an otherwise perfect night. But it was true, I did love her or at least it felt like love and I was glad to say it.

'Yes.'

Once again Netta flung her arms around my neck.

'And I love you too you silly boy.'

She loved me too? I knew she didn't mean it, but somehow that realisation didn't devalue the words themselves. And then Netta's tongue touched mine and we lost ourselves in kisses.

And the party raged all night. Everyone was drunk and high. Gabby was in his element, laughing, smiling, introducing people to one another, encouraging people to dance, eat and drink to excess, the perfect host. The band played on. A huge cake and candles were blown out, and from somewhere a sexy

Mayan stripper appeared and performed a scintillating dance that left absolutely nothing to the imagination.

'Tightest twat from here to Machu Picchu,' roared Gabby, his face red and sweating, but filled with joy. Sylvie and Netta watched in fascinated awe as the stunning Indian girl spread her legs so wide I thought they would snap. Netta shook her head and covered her eyes.

'No, it is not possible, surely they must break,' she said as she peeped between the fingers held across her eyes.

And the band played on. There were screams, shouts and glasses were dropped and food lay uneaten, and somebody even pissed in the hall. Dreamlike scenes flashed everywhere, shadows danced across the hacienda walls, hours disappeared into the void. At some point I observed Ronnie in the kitchen, deep in conversation with Gabby's friend Carlos. There was something I didn't like about Carlos. Somehow he made me uneasy and I made a mental note to question Ronnie about the discussion as soon as I got him alone. Then Netta grabbed my arm and pulled me into a bedroom. She locked the door behind her. I fell onto the bed. Netta was drunk and crazy, her eyes sparkling with desire and mischief. She tore off her dress in a blind fury. Then she stood there in the gloom of the room, naked, vibrant, and fabulous.

'Fuck me English boy!'

I pulled her towards me and we collapsed onto the bed. Netta flopped backwards and I looked at her lying there. This was it, the moment of moments, the reason for living and making one's way in the world. Netta looked directly into my eyes. I could feel my cock at the lips of her pussy, probing delicately. Netta arched her back and groaned...

-49-

Birds were singing, insects buzzing, a tropical dawn chorus. Netta was lying beside me, her eyes closed and peaceful. I would never spend another night with this girl. She and Sylvie were due to leave today. Then she would be gone, following another path in life and out of mine forever. And the question of where I would go and what would become of me remained valid, the answers shrouded in misty personal destiny. Maybe I would just drift away into infinity.

I was hot and dehydrated. The air in the room was close, filled with melancholy dreams and lost memories. I stumbled from the bed and into my shorts. I found my straw cowboy hat and plopped it on and went in search of another drink, for in my mind the party was far from over. Maybe I could party forever...

The hacienda was dead. Most partygoers had long since departed, but some remained asleep on settees and chairs, one or two crashed out on tiled floors. It was the morning after the party. I stumbled into the kitchen and found a bottle of beer. I flipped it open and took a swig. Outside daylight encroached upon the remains of the night, a fine and misty grey spreading far and wide. And somewhere off into the distance an imperceptible hint of magenta.

I wandered to the terrace. Evidence of a wild party was all around, smashed glasses, food, upturned chairs, shrivelled and forlorn streamers scattered across the extensive lawn.

I found a swinging sun chair and sat down.

The early morning scene was mysterious and portent. I imagined ancient Aztecs and Mayan warriors striding out before me, echoing down the years, a race of men and women now long gone. The call of the gecko sounded.

'It fades you know,' said a hushed and unexpected voice.

It was Gabby, dressed in silk pyjamas and swigging from a bottle of champagne, his face redder than ever and oddly bloated, his demeanour sad and lonesome.

'What fades?'

Gabby found a sun lounger and pulled it up beside mine. He collapsed into the chair with a great sigh.

'Youth, that's what Joseph. And it happens in the blinking of an eye. Look at me fat and red and old, but I wasn't always like this you know. I was once just like you. '

'Just like me?'

'Yes, believe it or not, I was handsome, young, dashing, possessor of a devil may care attitude. Had it all in the palm of my hand, but it's gone forever and now all I've got to look forward to is old age, physical disintegration and death.'

Death! Fuck, maybe Gabby was depressed or something? And would I one day be as old? An impossible suggestion, but everyone has to grow old, everyone has to die. It was just that the day seemed like a long, long way away. Maybe even in another galaxy or dimension.

'Everyone has to get old,' I said lamely.

Gabby swigged from the champagne bottle and burped.

'That's why you have to make the most of it kid, don't let life pass you by. That's what most people do, what they are most guilty of, merely existing instead of living. One has to bear in mind that there is only one shot at it. Do you remember what I said last night?'

'What's that Gabby?'

'Live everyday like it might just be your last.'

I tipped my cowboy hat upwards and took a pull from my beer bottle.

'I lived last night Gabby and I want to thank you once more

for inviting us to your great birthday bash. I, I mean we had a great time.'

'And the pretty bright thing, young Netta? Did you two get it on, now come on don't be coy.'

'Ha, well, yeah, we erm, we did.'

Gabby stood up, swigged the last of the champagne before chucking the bottle into the swimming pool where it landed with a resounding plop. Immediately, he opened another, the cork fizzing off into some distant bushes. He handed me a glass and filled it to over-flowing.

'That's what it's all about young man. For the sword outwears its sheath and the soul wears out the breast, and the heart must pause to breathe, and love itself have rest. And though the night was made for loving and the day returns too soon, yet we'll go no more a-roving by the light of the moon.'

'Shit, Gabby that's beautiful, did you just make that up?'

'And they say youth is wasted on the young. That Joseph was Lord Byron. Look at me, fifty years old and counting, yesterday a superstar now just another ordinary bum.'

'What d'ya mean? Look at this drum; you've got it made, like how did you get so rich?'

Gabby stared vacantly upon his beautifully manicured gardens.

'This,' he said, with a wicked laugh, 'it's a mirage young Joseph. Why the fuck do you think I'm living down here in the middle of nowhere? The global recession has done for me. I've lost everything and bankruptcy looms.'

I slurped the champagne and felt a boozy and wonderful hit.
'Fuck.'

'Yes, fuck indeed, but what the fuck does it matter? The sun will still be shining when they take me away.'

'Is it really that bad?'

'Damn right. The boom and the bust, and I'm busted.

'Are you serious Gabs?

'Oh don't worry. I've still got a few tricks up my sleeve. The bastards won't get me yet. More shampoo?'

I raised my glass and Gabby filled it to overflowing.

'Anyway let's not talk about my piffling troubles, tell me what your plans are. Are you and Ronnie staying on in Mexico?'

What were our plans? Did we intend to stay in Mexico? At that moment I would've loved to stay on in Mexico forever, but we were down to our last remaining bucks.

'We can't, we're running out of money. But we've got visas for Australia, we can work there.'

Gabby swigged his champers and appeared thoughtful.

'Yes Australia, the lucky country, a good choice. I'm sure you'll have a great time down under, but please promise that you'll spare a thought for me and old Mexico.'

'I'll never forget you Gabby or Mexico, especially the Beach of the Dead. You've been really generous, something I've never experienced from a total stranger. I'm gonna remember this night for the rest of my life.'

Gabby raised his glass.

'Let's make a toast, a toast to your future happiness in the land of the kangaroo.'

As our glasses clinked the rising sun broke free from the horizon and bathed Gabby's beautiful hacienda and verdant jungle garden in dazzling yellow sunbeams. We sat in silence. Three little birds appeared on the terrace and bobbed around. I studied the flowers, the beautiful colours.

'Great day,' I said.

There was no response. I glanced to Gabby. He was fast asleep and older than ever.

-50-

Outside Gabby's hacienda, a truck was ready and waiting. It was late now and the girls didn't have time to hang around. I felt blue. Maybe it was because of what Gabby had told me about growing old. Or maybe it was because nothing appeared to be what it actually was. Not Ronnie, Netta, Gabby, Mexico, even the Huts of the Lost Elation. Appearances can be deceptive. The truck took us all the way back to the beach.

Me and Ronnie sat in Penelope's and nursed a couple of cold beers. Juanita acted strangely sullen and barely acknowledged our presence. I peeled the label off my bottle of beer.

'I'm gonna miss the girls,' I said.

'You mean you're gonna miss Netta's pussy.'

'Don't be vulgar.'

'Don't be what?'

'I'm serious, I'm gonna miss those girls, miss their company.'

'I know what you mean.'

'You do?'

'Yeah, I do, we've had fun, and life is meant to be fun isn't it?'

I gazed at the beach and the ocean. A dispirited dog trotted past, tail between its legs. We would be leaving as well. Australia. I wondered what would happen there, how we would get along. Then I thought about work. I didn't want to work. I wanted to just lie in a hammock and watch the world go by. In my mind a responsible life or even so called reality was overrated and outdated.

An hour later the girls appeared. A taxi had been ordered. Their enormous backpacks made them look like hermit crabs. We sat in Penelope's and talked for a while until Netta gave me the signal. We went for a final walk along the beach, splashing in the shallows, a thin embroidery of foam cascading across our feet as we walked across dark sand.

'I'm glad I met you Joseph,' said Netta, 'you're a good guy.'

Netta was a sweet-hearted girl, a gentle soul without ulterior motives or bad intentions, just happy to live life to the full and have some fun before she grew old. I knew I'd miss her or an image of her.

'I'll remember you forever.'

Netta stopped walking.

'You will?'

'Of course I will, how could I ever forget?'

Back at Penelope's the taxi was waiting, a driver shoving the gargantuan backpacks into the boot of the car. Ronnie and Sylvie were kissing. It was time to say goodbye. Netta gave me another kiss. We promised to meet up again. The girls jumped into the back of the cab and waved. The sound of fond farewells filled the air and then the car drove away, up the dusty track and around a bend...

51

The hammock outside Shangri-La was swinging and I was inside. Ronnie was busy mixing the Peyote concoction, sticking strictly to the instructions given to us by the Kaleidoscope Kid.

'What did he say again one part peyote, two parts water?'

My thoughts were focused on Netta and the party, the pool, the sea, her naked body against mine, the breasts, thighs, pussy...

'Yay something like that or it could've been the other way around.'

'Don't you remember?'

I remembered Netta's smile, her beautiful hair and blue, blue eyes.

'Er, no, well I remember the Kid said there was enough there for sixteen eight hour trips.'

'Okay, as we want more than an eight hour trip I'll double the dose. And erm, just to be on the safe side I'll triple it.'

I stopped thinking about Netta.

'Just to be on the safe side?'

Ronnie chuckled.

'We're gonna be at the beach all day and long into the night, maybe even 48hrs so it needs to be strong.'

I jumped out of the hammock and paced the ledge.

'But what if it's too strong, what if we flip out, do a Syd Barrett or Peter Green and never come back.'

'What, like lose it permanently?'

'Yeah, lose it, go AWOL, Missing in Action, away with the fairies. It's happened before.' Ronnie held up the bag containing the pulped cactus.

'But it's just a plant, hundred percent natural. How can

something natural harm you? We'll sip a bit at a time. If it becomes too powerful, we'll just stop taking it and focus on chilling.'

Peyote - taken as a drug in ceremonial rituals by Native American Indians for thousands of years - was not something to be blasé about. Most Mesoamerican cultures considered it sacred. Surely a sacred thing could not harm you mentally? I wasn't sure, there was always human frailty to consider, a dodgy gene, and unexpected freak-outs. And peyote contained mescaline, a powerful hallucinogenic, similar in properties to L.S.D. I recalled lurid descriptions of such narcotic experiences by some of my favourite authors. Aldous Huxley and *The Doors of Perception* - Jack Kerouac in *On the Road* - William Burroughs in *The Yage Letters* and Tom Wolfe's *Kool-Aid Acid Test*. Over the years I'd digested a good deal of psychedelic literature as well as psychedelics and the inherent dangers associated with such practices were within the sphere of my knowledge. And yet for every downside there was always an upside. A dope-fiend had to take their chances - for if one didn't test their own individual mental capacity then one couldn't say they were truly awakened as a human being.

Ronnie handed me a cup.

'Banish all negative thoughts and think positive. This could be interesting - could be like no drug we've ever experienced before. Get ready for a total derangement of the senses.'

'I'm ready. Hopefully we'll access some of our phylogenetic memory that Burroughs talked about in *The Yage Letters*.'

'That's right, that's right - thee old collective unconscious - it's time to get in touch with our ancestors and seek some illumination.'

I took the cup and we raised a toast. Then Ronnie made a speech.

'We are gathered here today to relinquish our humble spirit to the greater spirit. We acknowledge the power of the sacred cactus and ask that no harm come to either of us. Now let's drink.'

With that I downed some of the peyote concoction. The taste was bitter.

'Just close your eyes and force it down in one gulp,' ordered Ronnie.

I took another swig; it tasted just as bad if not worse, but somehow it stayed down.

'Come on let's head to the little cove before the effects kick in. What are you gonna do during the trip?'

I picked up my little knapsack, inside of which was food and firewood, a bottle of water, notepad and pencil.

'Gonna write one hundred beach poems.'

Ronnie grabbed his knapsack and pulled out a sheet of paper.

'Good thinking and I'm gonna sculpt one of the glyphs of the ancient Aztec calendar, the Wind God.'

I studied the paper in Ronnie's hand. There were several drawings all depicting the same strange and wonderful character.

'Wow, that is one freaky looking dude and intricate, but it's a great idea.'

'Come on let's go, no time to lose.'

We set off down the jungle path, past the Starlight Hotel sign where Freddie the Iguana was standing guard as usual, basking in the early morning sun.

'Morning Fred,' said Ronnie as we passed.

Freddie didn't move.

The sky was overcast and the atmosphere unnaturally still, not a puff of breeze to rustle a palm frond. The ocean was flat, no roaring surf, no waves or white horses, just a sensual swaying motion with ripples caressing the shore.

'I've never seen the sea so calm.'

Ronnie looked around.

'Like the calm before the storm.'

I gazed upon the far horizon. Heaviness resided in the air, oppressive and close, stultifying. We walked on. We climbed the rocks at the far end of the beach and scrambled down to the isolated and wild cove we'd identified all those days before. Then we built a camp on the sand and lit a small fire. We faced the ocean and waited for something to happen. Twenty minutes, maybe thirty went by, and nothing. Everything remained remarkably still. All the sea did was sway. It felt odd. I looked at Ronnie.

'Maybe we should drink another cup?' he suggested.

I recalled an old Zen lunatic mantra and recited it aloud.

'When walking just walk, when sitting just sit, most of all don't wobble.'

Ronnie smiled. 'Lin Chi, Zen master, here drink this.'

I took the cup and downed the contents in one. The mixture tasted as foul as before. I grimaced, gagged.

'Your turn,' I croaked.

Ronnie adopted a determined demeanour and raised his cup. A philosophical expression adorned his visage. Then he downed the peyote and casually tossed the empty cup over his shoulder.

'Nice,' he said through gritted teeth.

We sat and waited.

After an hour Ronnie said he was going to sculpt his ancient glyph in the sand, The Wind God, Ehecatl-Quetzalcoatl, and he relocated to a far corner of the cove. I pulled out my notepad and pencil and wrote a title on the page: *Beach Poem #1*. It was then that it hit, blinding transformations, altered perceptions. I closed my eyes. It was all too beautiful. Brilliant colours and patterns flashed behind my eyelids. The sound of limitless oceans exploded onto the frontiers of the four major lobes of my cerebral cortex - small waves crashing onto rocks sounding like intelligible words. The ocean was communicating with me. It was primordial and predestined. Everything faded away, images, scenery, everything. I was spinning through time and space surrounded by immensities of silence. The beach had become the universe and the universe the beach. The rest of the world disappeared into the ether.

I walked over to Ronnie.

'It's happening,' I said.

Ronnie flinched and staggered backwards. 'Yeah, it is - whoa, easy, easy.'

'What?'

'Fucking hell - just had a mad one there.'

'Like what?'

'I'm talking out of body experience.'

'Groovy.'

'Wait till you ave one.'

'For now I'm not scared or paranoid just content to know that one-day I'm going to die and it's okay. I feel good about it. Look at the ocean spray and hear what it is saying. It is telling me that it is as old as the earth itself. That is reality, a wave crashing onto the rocks. When we die the waves will still be washing the shore and that's all there is to it. There's no need to worry about anything because everything looks after itself.'

Ronnie returned to his sculpture.

'I thought you were gonna write some beach poems - whoa another one there!'

I dipped my feet in the sea and waved my arms. 'Poetry-schmoetry,' I yelled into the atmosphere.

I skipped to the other end of the little cove and sat on a rock. I watched Ronnie sculpting. He worked at a furious pace, only stopping to scrutinise his drawings or look around as if someone or something was there, and then back to it. I pulled out my notepad and faced the ocean. There was no wind or even a breeze. The sky remained overcast.

Weird visuals afflicted me as I began to write. The poems came one after the other, two, three, four, five, ten, eleven, twelve. I didn't bother with titles. At *Beach Poem #37* I stopped. I was no longer able to continue. The letters began re-arranging themselves forming lines that were nothing more than gibberish. Some sort of mental disintegration was taking hold. I wasn't sure how long I'd been writing. As things took a sudden and darker turn I became convinced that there were other worlds out there and that man wasn't alone in the universe. Man, I was peaking. I started hallucinating - intense sexual images flashed before my mind's eye - graphic and terrible. Random men fucked random women whilst mutilating themselves. There were images of flagellation, bondage, and cannibalism. I fell from the rock and dropped to the sand. I stared up to the sky, terrified. Gruesome images continued unabated, entire civilisations crumbling before me. I picked up a pebble and studied it. There was a world inside the pebble, men and woman trapped, screaming for help, for me to help, but how the fuck could I help? We were all trapped. I tossed the pebble containing the other world into the sea. The screams continued for a while and then petered out. I threw myself onto the beach whereupon every granule of sand came alive. The grains had tiny eyes, legs and mouths. I left my body and floated into the upper regions of the sky beyond the clouds. Everything was beautiful again. I roamed some heavenly gardens, hanging like Babylon while down below my mortal body writhed in agony - my face etched with misery. Faces paraded before me, evil visages from past millennia. I wondered when it would all end. My life, this bad trip. Oh God was this a bad trip and what if this bad trip lasted forever? The phrase - Go Ask Alice - repeated itself over and over in my head until I laughed hysterically. What was real and unreal - or were both states equally the same? I grew calmer and wondered who I was. Then, gradually, the intensity of the high, if it could be called a high, subsided and some sort of normality re-inserted itself within my core.

How much time had passed, seconds or centuries? I looked over to Ronnie, his sculpture was by now huge, the size of a small car. I jumped from the rock and dashed over. Brilliant flashes of colour appeared around the periphery of my vision, red, greens, blue, yellows, the colours flashed from the ends of my hands and feet and mesmerised me. I was electrified!

Ronnie stepped back from his sculpture. He was drenched in sweat.

'Whaddya think?'

'It's fucking amazing man.'

Ronnie wiped the sweat from his brow. 'Are you getting visuals?'

'Yeah, flashing bright colours. I'm calm now, but it got intense back there.'

'Yeah, I saw.'

'You saw?'

'You were acting pretty strange, talking to yourself, rolling around on the sand and shit.'

'I lost it back there.'

'It's a powerful experience with three stages. The middle stage is the darkest or most bizarre. During the middle stage of the trip I experienced some sort of past life regression.'

217

'You did?'

'Yeah, it was fucked up. I was the head of some sort of ordinary family - the Dad. I worked as a bus driver and had a wife and three children. I hated the wife.'

'How long have we been tripping, how long has all this lasted? I glimpsed other worlds.'

Ronnie counted his fingers. 'By my estimation, we've already been here three days.'

'What the fuck?'

'Well, I was with the family for three days. On the second day I had an argument with my wife, which became violent.'

This shit, which Ronnie was feeding me, was too strange. 'Where was the family, where did they live?'

'In England between the wars. After the fight my wife refused to speak to me. Then the sculpture came alive.'

'The sculpture came alive?'

Ronnie pointed to the sand. 'This one here. The 1930s family disappeared and Old Ehecatl materialised before me. He floated above my head and off towards the horizon, speaking in tongues.'

'Mother.'

'It was like by sculpting his image or representation so faithfully I've invoked his spirit. And have you noticed the wind has picked up?'

A stiff breeze buffeted my face. Clouds of sand flailed across the beach. As for the sea it had been whipped into frenzy, a million white horses appearing out of nowhere, and on the horizon a vast bank of angry black cloud hovered ominously.

'Jesus Christ, where the fuck did they come from?'

'I think I've awakened the spirit of the Wind God.'

'Is that good or bad?'

'I'm not sure.'

The winds grew faster and stronger. The nimbus accelerated in our direction. The heavens opened. It rained, heavily and violently. The sand moved, tremulous and fantastic like a shape shifter.

Ronnie tapped my arm. 'What do ya think the family represented?'

'Right now I'm more worried about the approaching weather. Look into the middle of it there. That's the eye of the fucking storm!'

'I think you're right. The family must mean something, but this is not the time or place for any in-depth psychedelic analysis. I just hope those weird images don't come back to haunt me.'

'Come back to haunt you?'

Ronnie looked at me oddly. 'The sins of the father.'

'Er?'

'By no means will the almighty clear the guilty, visiting the iniquity of the fathers on the children and the children's children, to the third and the fourth generation.'

'Is that from the Bible?'

'Exodus.'

I eyeballed the weather. 'And speaking of Exodus - I think it's time we embarked upon one of our own.'

Everything happened fast. Darkness flooded the land like a river of night. The wind howled and screamed. Forked lightning flashed and darted from cloud to sea, followed by rolling thunderclaps. The rain lashed the beach and cliffs. Ronnie's sculpture was obliterated.

'We'd better get back to the huts,' Ronnie roared.

'Yeah,' I shouted.

We made our way to the bottom of the cliffs, heads bowed to ferocious and wicked winds. The sea level had risen dramatically, barring access to the lower footholds. Streams of water cascaded down the cliffs in newly formed torrents.

'Shit,' said Ronnie.

'Fuck, what we gonna do?'

'It's either wait out the storm or climb in treacherous conditions.'

'I say climb.'

'Let's go.'

We climbed. The storm raged. Somehow we scrambled to the top without being swept or blown away. From the ridge, the thin strip of sand leading to the Beach of the Dead was nothing but foaming ocean.

'We're gonna ave to swim.' yelled Ronnie.

'Let's do it!' I screamed.

We scrambled down the rocks, towards the smashing waves. We looked at each other and dived head first. Immediately I was dragged under and rolled over and over until my lungs were ready to burst. This is it I thought, the end, Nirvana.

Then, amazingly, I touched the seabed and rose to my feet bursting into the atmosphere, gasping for air, but alive. The beach was within touching distance.

Exhausted, I flung myself to shore with my last remaining strength, lying on the wet sand fighting for breath, white foam all around.

I propped myself up on my elbows.

Where was Ronnie?

Just then Miguel appeared, naked, his long curly locks blowing in the wind. He looked like Jesus Christ. Fuck, maybe he was the saviour? I pointed towards the raging ocean.

'Miguel, Ronnie, my friend, need help.'

Miguel strode into the sea. I found the strength to stand upright and peer into the raging torrents. I couldn't see anything or anyone. I prayed to the gods, all the gods, any god. Then they appeared, Miguel first, with Ronnie dragged behind. They reached the beach and collapsed to the sand.

'Ronnie?' I cried.

Ronnie choked and gurgled, gasping for air. Seawater emerged from his mouth in surprising quantities.

'Thought I was gone,' he spluttered.

Miguel marched back out to sea.

'Where ya going?' I asked.

'This, amigo, is the best time to swim.'

'Are you crazy?'

'All you have to do is go with the flow,' cried Miguel, before diving under.

For a few moments his head bobbed up and down and then nothing. Ronnie grabbed me by the shoulder.

'Come on, we need to get to the huts, find shelter.'

We rose shakily to our feet. We found the path and inched our way along. Tremendous winds pinned us to the cliff face. After an eternity we made it to the huts and tumbled into Cool Breeze. Somehow I was able to shut the rickety door.

52

Ronnie placed a couple of beer crates against the door. Outside, the storm raged and the wind whistled hysterically. I found a couple of lukewarm beers in the ice-chest. The noise was deafening, unbelievable.

'You'll need it for the nerves,' I shouted.

Ronnie took the bottle. 'I had another mother-fucking epiphany out there,' he shouted.

'Yeah?'

'Thought I was a gonna and there he was, Jesus Christ fucking Superstar.'

'You mean Miguel?'

'Fucker saved my life.'

'He went back out there.'

'Crazy shit.'

'What're we gonna do?'

'Hole up here till the storm blows over.'

The rickety walls of the hut shook and creaked, ready to be blown away at any moment. I got scared and from the look of it so did Ronnie. There were only four beers left. We drank them. It made us feel better. Ronnie spoke.

'We've got no money left.'

'I know, what's the plan?'

'There is no plan.'

I burst out laughing.

'That's the first time you've never had a plan.'

'Well I don't have one right now.'

'I think that's a sign.'

'A sign of what?'

'That it's time to go home.'

Ronnie eyed me evilly. 'No way, we're never going home. There has to be an answer, an alternative to what I've already got lined up.'

'What have you got lined up?'

'Forget it, but we're not going home, no matter what.'

'Ah come on, we can go home, regroup and hit the road again.'

Ronnie's face darkened. It lasted a second, a millisecond or eternity. Then he exploded.

'Fuck you. You're a fucking burden, a liability, always have been always will be. From now on I go it alone. I DON'T NEED ANYONE!'

I saw Ronnie in an entirely unique light then, right there, high up on that remote jungle ledge in Mexico. My friend would do anything in the pursuit of freedom, anything necessary to continue the search for the lost elation, with or without me. Yet there had to be limits. How far does one take it? Freedom, what the fuck was it anyway, wasn't one trap just replaced with another? The search for the lost elation, to non-confirm, to drop out. And what did he mean by the sins of the father? Ronnie screamed into my face.

'I CAN GO ANYWHERE. I'LL DO IT ALL BY MYSELF. ALL THE WAY MOTHERFUCKER, CENTRAL AMERICA, BRAZIL, CHILE, PERU, ARGENTINA. AND I WON'T STOP THERE. I'LL FUCKING HIT ANTARCTICA!'

Ronnie appeared to have finally lost his mind. 'And then what, become a snow gypsy carving mad sculptures in the ice?

'YEAH, AND I'LL...' but before Ronnie could finish a stupendous thunder clap and sparkling blue flash threw him clean across the floor of the hut. This was followed by an almighty rumbling and terrifying cracking. Moments later the door of the hut flung open and the wind rushed in like a torpedo.

'What the fuck was that?'

Ronnie edged towards the door. I followed close behind. We took a tentative peek outside. It was like a vision of hell, Dante's inferno, the second circle of the Divine Comedy. Howling winds, driving rain, zero visibility. There was no sign of Shangri-la, no washing table, gramophone, hammocks, just the smashed trunk of a great palm tree and grotesquely twisted fronds. Ronnie tried to close the flimsy door of the hut, but it was useless, the wood ripped from his despairing hands.

'WE'LL HAVE TO GO DOWN,' HE SCREAMED.

'I THOUGHT YOU WERE GOING IT ALONE!' I SCREAMED.

Ronnie smiled a gruesome smile. 'We're in this together remember, right to the bitter end.'

I staggered over and put a trembling arm around his shoulder and he put an arm around mine. We both looked at each other before stepping out onto the ledge and into the abyss...

53

I awoke to seagulls crying and waves crashing. I opened one eye. The sky had been washed, pure, clean, and amazingly blue. The hurricane had blown itself out and aside from a cool breeze, all was calm. It was the aftermath.

As for the Beach of the Dead, it was gone, along with the Hut of the Lost Elation and the Starlight Hotel. Somehow, we had made it to the bottom of the cliff and found refuge in the wreckage of Penelope's Cabana. Juanita was nowhere to be seen and neither was anyone else for that matter - it was a ghost beach. I wondered about the fate of Miguel. Surely he was drowned, not even a superman could survive in that tempest. I scanned the beach, of which only a thin strip of sand remained. The huts and restaurants had been flattened, toppled like a flimsy pack of cards. A lone dog trotted the sand.

Ronnie lifted his sodden head from the sand and rose slowly to his feet. 'We got out just in time.'

I stood up and brushed wet sand, seaweed, shells, driftwood and other beach debris from my clothes and skin.

'What we gonna do?' I asked.

Ronnie pulled a dead fish from his hair, inspected it, and then tossed it to the ground.

'I've got an idea,' he said.

'Such as?'

'We take Carlos up on his offer.'

'What offer?'

'Ten thousand will be enough to get us to South America and continue our travels for another year at least.'

I watched a lone cloud float across the horizon. The cloud was remarkable in its own way. Ronnie was talking in riddles.

His heterochromic eyes were ablaze, just like they were when he invented the idea of robbing a bank another lifetime ago. I avoided eye to eye contact - that's where his power lay. If Ronnie stared at you in that way of his, you had the feeling that you were being magnetised, or that he was about to rob you of your will.

'What the fuck are you talking about?'

'I'm talking about getting our hands on some filthy lucre amigo and then more travels.'

'But how?'

'Easy as one two three. I've got it all figured out. One of us sucks his cock while the other two search for the money.'

'Suck whose cock?'

'Gabby's.'

Ronnie was on a roll and my mind was swimming.

'Gabby's?'

'That's right, that's right. Gabby's sweet cock. Carlos gave me the low down the night of the party at the Hacienda. That rich fuck keeps ten thousand hidden away for a rainy day.'

'Are you outta of your fucking mind? Gabby's been nothing but a hundred percent nice to us, and yet here you are talking about robbing the fucker. Get a fucking grip.'

Ronnie shook free from my grasp and paced the sand. 'You get a fucking grip. We're down to our last pesos and without cash we're fucked. Gabby's a nice guy, but he'll survive without the money, whereas in all possibility we fucking won't. It's survival of the fittest, each man to his own, and to my mind a justifiable re-distribution of wealth.'

'Bullshit! And no way am I sucking anyone's cock, let alone Gabby's.'

'Let him suck your cock then,' suggested Ronnie.

I couldn't believe what I was hearing. Maybe Ronnie had finally flipped? All the signs of mental deterioration were clearly evident. His recklessness more than a little freaky, yet in the interim I didn't know what to do except go along with his nuttiness.

'We toss a coin on it.'

'Bullshit.'

'It's a small sacrifice to pay.'

'When do we toss?'

Ronnie pulled out a peso.

'Right fucking now.'

As the coin tumbled into the air, I began formulating strategies to stop my best friend endangering my liberty with all this nonsense.

'Heads,' I said.

And of course heads it wasn't.

With that decided Ronnie discussed the job in hand, outlining the crazed shit in detail. He told a good story. The rumour was that Gabby kept a stash of around ten thousand dollars hidden in his hacienda at all times. According to Carlos a safe was concealed in one of the bedrooms.

'Come on let's go there now.'

'Go where now?'

Ronnie began walking away. 'To the road where Carlos is waiting.'

'You mean this shit has already been decided?'

Ronnie had some of the peyote left, some green globules rescued from his shorts. He munched on some and handed me the remnants, 'Of course it fucking has. As soon as Carlos gave me the low down, I knew it was just too good an opportunity to miss, and would also get us out of the pickle we currently find ourselves in.'

I took the peyote remnants and necked them. 'And what if I hadn't agreed to the plan?'

Ronnie looked over, staring at me with great intensity and I knew I was doomed. 'That outcome was not included in the equation.'

'Great.'

When we reached the road sure enough there he was, Carlos, waiting in a parked Nissen. Once again I didn't like the look of him. He was another Eyes Down, a certifiable wrong un. Ronnie jumped into the passenger seat, while I took the back. Carlos was in an excitable and irritable state. Jumpy. He started the engine and tore off down the road, driving erratically. Ronnie outlined the plan a final time.

'Si dis cock-sucking is goo idea amigo,' said Carlos.

Ronnie's eyes were wild, all forms of self-control cast aside in an excited state of feverish abandonment. '

'And while Senor Homo is otherwise detained we take the money and run.'

Carlos massaged the steering wheel, his black eyes sparkling with greed. 'Si, is spoken. Once de money we have I drive joo de border. In Guatemala joo safe.'

It was straightforward. Nobody knew our identity, where we came from, or where we were going. Travelers arrived and left The Beach of the Dead every day. We would be just another couple of gringos disappearing into the sticky Mexican void.

When we reached the hacienda, Carlos parked some way from the drive and told us to wait by the vehicle. It was broad daylight.

'Shit, somehow I don't trust that Carlos character,' I said.

Ronnie produced a metal bar from his shorts. 'Neither do I, that's why I'm tooled up, make sure he doesn't get any funny ideas.'

I eyeballed the bar in Ronnie's hands.

'I don't want any violence.'

'This is just in case of an emergency, or as a last resort.'

'And then there's the blow-job aspect, what if I can't go through with it?'

'Just think of fucking Netta naked in the surf or those fabulous breasts you saw on the beach every day for the last few weeks.'

Ten or twenty minutes passed until Carlos reappeared and beckoned us with an urgent hand motion. We approached in silence.

'Everything is goo. The ole man inside. He suspect nothing.'

We entered Gabby's drive and approached the entrance to the Hacienda. I recalled some random events from the great party of a few nights before. Feelings of guilt imposed themselves on my tormented mind. In no way did Gabby deserve what he was going to get, but it appeared he was going to get it anyway. Fuck it, it was only money.

We walked straight into the house and entered the living area. Gabby was seated on a sprawling, blanket covered settee. He looked tired, worn out, like an old man.

'How's it going Gabby?' asked Ronnie casually.

'Better for seeing you two alive and well, that I must confess. That hurricane was a nasty business, completely destroyed my gardens and pool.'

'We got out by the skin of our teeth,' I said.

'In that case refreshments are the order of the day. Now what would you like to drink?'

'A beer would be good,' replied Ronnie with a grin.

'I propose something a little stronger, tequila?'

'Okay, no lime.'

'And for you young Joseph?'

'Same.'

'Carlos?'

Carlos nodded blankly, his face expressionless.

Once Gabby mixed the drinks, we sat around drinking and making small talk. Carlos had already told Gabby I was up for a little homo fun in exchange for three hundred dollars. According to Carlos I was in desperate need of the money so I could fly to Australia and look for work. In the strange set of circumstances we found ourselves in it all seemed plausible.

After two more rounds of drinks I began to loosen up. Maybe it wasn't such a crazy idea after all, and maybe Ronnie was right. Gabby would survive without the money and we would get to continue our travels for another year or so. Nobody would get hurt.

I drank a couple of chilled beers and chased them with more tequila. I was quickly boozy. Gabby relaxed. All feelings of guilt at my treacherous behaviour evaporated. I got up and wandered into the bedroom as planned. Gabby was there moments later. Then it was just Gabby and me, alone together. I gave the old fag the once over. He was balding, red-faced, and overweight. And the creased linen suit and designer sunglasses hardly helped. I shuddered. Then thoughts of South America flitted through my mind, Brazil, Rio De Janeiro, The Girl from Ipanema.

'Get me another Dos Equis and a double Hornitos, I feel like getting loaded.'

Gabby smiled. 'After last night's traumatic experience its the only way forward I'm afraid.'

While Gabby fetched more drinks I contemplated the situation a final time.

What if there wasn't any cash on the premises? What if Carlos had set us up? What if we all got arrested and thrown into a filthy Mexican jail?

When Gabby returned I downed the drinks he handed me in huge gulps.

230

Then I faced up to my responsibility. I sat down on the bed and pulled off my shorts.

'I fancy a blow-job.'

Gabby's face went redder than it already was and beads of sweat popped out on his forehead. 'Oh good God boy, are you sure, I mean you're comfortable with this?'

'Yeah, I am, but first turn off the lights.'

By now I was drunk to high heaven. I closed my eyes. My cock entered something warm and soft. I thought of all the naked girls on the beach and imagined screwing, sucking, and fucking each and every one of them. I visualised breasts, thighs and cunts. I had to hand it to the old fuck. He had an effective technique. When it came right down to it, a mouth was just another mouth, wet and willing, masculine or feminine, in the end it all amounted to the same thing...

When I opened my eyes Gabby was on his knees, taking everything I had to offer, lapping it all up.

'That's it baby; give me all of it, all in my fucking face.'

A sickening sense of revulsion overwhelmed me. I pushed Gabby away and pulled up my ripped shorts.

'Get the fuck away from me you dirty old cunt.'

Gabby touched his lips. A large blob of spunk coated his chin like a white beard.

'Why you ungrateful little...'

Then somebody hit the lights and an unseen force wrestled me to the ground...

I awoke to find Ronnie dragging me out of the hacienda by my ankles.

'What the fuck are you doing?'

Ronnie looked down at me, surprised. 'Can you walk?'

'I think so.'

'Get up then, we're out of here, el fucking pronto.'

I stood up, unsteadily. Ronnie wiped his sweaty brow.

'You were right not to trust Carlos. He couldn't wait, a loose fucking canon.'

'What the fuck happened?'

'Carlos lost the plot, tried to kill the pair of you. I got there just in the nick of time.'

'What about Gabby?'

'Out cold same as Carlos, but they won't stay that way forever, now move it.'

'What the fuck we gonna do?'

'Get the fuck out of the fucking country a.s.a.p.'

'Jesus Christ!'

Ronnie pulled a wedge of cash from his pants.

'I found the fucking money though and there's a lot more than ten grand that's for sure...'

-54-

As we drove to the border Ronnie told me his version of what had happened in the hacienda.

'When Carlos couldn't locate the cash, he went mental, shouting and cursing out Gabby. I was in another room when I heard the commotion. By the time I got there Gabby and you were out cold.'

'We were?'

'Fucking right and Carlos was holding a blade about to slit your throats. I had no other option, but to cosh the prick. It was funny the way he dropped.'

I wondered if I was dreaming.

How had he found the money? In the kitchen. Why hadn't Carlos found it? He missed it. These were Ronnie's answers. Something didn't add up. We were sure to get caught and sent to prison.

It was a long and lonely drive to the border between Mexico and Guatemala. I kept waiting for the police to show and arrest us. Gabby and Carlos were bound to have come round and called law enforcement hours ago. Ronnie outlined plans for further travel and adventure in Central and South America. He was energised and full of life, possessor of a clear conscience. The atmosphere was surreal.

At the border we were asked to show our passports to the authorities and issued with transit visas. I tried to act normal, but internally I was a mess. I no longer wanted to travel anywhere. I wanted to go home and forget everything. In contrast Ronnie acted like nothing had happened; displaying a disconcerting insouciance to all external events. It was perplexing.

As we drove further into the hot sticky jungle night, along empty Guatemalan roads, I considered the situation.

Were Gabby and Carlos still alive? Ronnie said he would do anything to continue his travels, anything to avoid going home. Yet how far do you push in pursuit of freedom, what lengths will you go to? Was it possible my best friend had topped Gabby and Carlos in exchange for freedom to continue his journey? And if so was it possible he felt morally justified in his actions?

I was scared. If Ronnie had laid down two men, what was to stop him from murdering another? I recalled his bizarre moral viewpoint on the hypothetical rape of Sylvie, the ominous words during the hurricane. I had become a liability, a burden, someone he could live without. The sins of the father. I wasn't sure if I knew Ronnie any longer, but does anyone get to know anyone, really, I mean the real them?

Ronnie outlined his future plans.

'Further man, further - that's where we go and we keep going. If we run out of money we find a way of getting hold of some more. No one knows who we are or where we're going. We'll be masterminds of the road and our life will be lived like one never-ending adventure story. There will be more girls, new people, places and things to see and do. Think of it - me and you - experiencing a never-ending series of life firsts...

The car kept going - driven by a madman - devouring those white lines in the middle of the road, and ahead the road went on forever - into the night - onwards, always onwards...

Burrito Deluxe
by Joseph Ridgwell

First published in 2015 by
Leamington Books
46 Leamington Terrace
Edinburgh

ISBN 978 0 9932272 02
Cover by Jose Arroyo
Set in Cambria
Printed by Bell & Bain Ltd, Glasgow